# PASSAGE

# PASSAGE

A NOVEL BY
## DEAN FULLER

DODD, MEAD & COMPANY
New York

1   2   3   4   5   6   7   8   9   10

Library Of Congress Cataloging in Publication Data
Fuller, Dean.
    Passage.

    I. Title.
PS3556.U38P3   1983      813'.54         82-23665
ISBN 0-396-08134-7

To my Father

# PART ONE

# SANDWICH

# CHAPTER 1

The watch supervisor at Coast Guard Comcenter, Governor's Island, sat at the duty desk and sipped his coffee. He still had a short stack of routine Search and Rescue reports to go through. Basically, though, it had been a quiet night. He was thinking about french toast and crisp bacon when the Distress Traffic Telex went off. He moved quickly to the Siemans machine and watched the communication appear line by line.

FM: CRCC HALIFAX

TO: USCG RCC NYK

BT

ST. JOHN'S RADIO/VON RECEIVED FOLLOWING 281148 Z JUN FROM
*M/V BEARN*/FAPZ, SOCIETE DE TRANSPORT MARITIME:

QUOTE. ATTEMPTED SALVAGE SAILYACHT *HOUND OF ULSTER*, APPROX 11 METRES, 0812 Z 350 NM E ST. JOHN'S NFLD 46-36N X 44-06W.

NO ONE ABOARD. NO ONE ABOARD. NO ONE ABOARD.

REMOVED LOG AND TAPE CASSETTES.

UNABLE TOW SPEED REQ MAKE ETA 30 JUNE 5PM. ABANDONED IN FOG 1130Z, 47N X 44-07W. UNQUOTE.

SIGNED, G. CASTAIGN, MASTER.

BT

The Watch Supervisor dialed 7055. A voice came back immediately.

"Rescue Coordinating Center, Lieutenant Quinn."

"I got a hot SAR for you," said the Supervisor.

Within thirty seconds Lieutenant Quinn had the Telex and was transferring the coordinates of the abandoned yacht to the Center's ceiling-to-floor wall chart of the Atlantic coast of North America. He marked the position with a red magnetic plate.

He then walked across the hall to Comcenter, called AMVER and requested a computer surface picture of all merchant vessels within four hundred miles of the distress coordinates. While he was waiting for the Surpic to come back he returned to his turret, dialed Halifax RCC and requested an Argus aircraft be placed on standby at Gander.

"Yachting in the bloody North Atlantic!" said the Canadian coordinator. "Probably one of those single-handed chaps. There ought to be a law!"

Lieutenant Quinn established that the Canadians had a ninety-footer at St. John's which would be operational within forty-eight hours. The nearest USCG cutter was *Acushnet* in Portland. He thanked CRCC and hung up.

As a matter of course, Quinn filed the yacht's name, length overall and last known position with North Atlantic Air Traffic Control. He also filed a Department of Transportation memo with Documentation and Inspection.

The AMVER Surpic came back. Quinn selected six vessels—four inbound and two outbound along the northern great circle

4

route—whose courses would bring them closest to *Hound of Ulster* within twenty-four hours. They were contacted by Code (CW) on the call tape from Radio Station NMF, Boston.

Finally, Lieutenant Quinn filed the item with Notice to Mariners. At 0850, less than an hour after the emergency traffic had been received at Coast Guard HQ, a special XXX Distress Bulletin was issued on short wave from NMF, Boston, to all ships north of 41°N and west of 60°W.

In the Weather Bureau at Rockefeller Center, Chaim Gold, the bureau's surface analyst, was listening to Lazar Berman play Rachmaninoff's Third Concerto on WQXR while trying to out-guess a weak low in the Ohio valley. During the slow movement, his Atlas shortwave radio, which monitored the emergency frequency continuously, started yammering. Chaim heard "Hound of Ulster" and "No one aboard" and "Abandoned." He went to the phone and called his ex-roommate at Truly's Boatyard in Sandwich, Connecticut.

# CHAPTER 2

Roger Truly, like most boatyard owners, never intended to own a boatyard. He had expected to be an architect with solar-heated offices in a black skyscraper. But, after four years in the NATO Navy and a disastrous four-month marriage to a dippy Russian dancer, he ended up in the art department of a New York ad agency designing cigarette packages and trucking-company logos. He loathed it. On weekends, he helped his father, Spencer, run the Sandwich Marine Service. The weekends got longer. Finally, when his father semiretired, Roger, then twenty-nine, mortgaged everything, bought the business and changed the name to Truly's Boatyard.

The phone clicked. In a moment, Chaim heard the double ring

that always made him homesick for New England. Barbara Foster answered.

"Truly's."

"It's the weatherjew," said Chaim.

Barbara giggled. "Listen," she said, "when are you going to pack your wok and come cook us Chinese?"

"Soon. How about carp in chicken fat?"

"Revolting. I'll call Roger."

Barbara yelled out the window. Roger and the head rigger were putting a new rod forestay in a PJ 43. Roger picked up the dockside phone and greeted his old roommate.

"Are you returning my call of last year?"

"I got lousy news, Roger," Chaim said. He told him what he'd just heard on SW.

Roger felt the warmth of the sun on his back and watched the soft morning light move down the maple trees lining Griswold Street. He was silent. He simply couldn't grasp a thing for which he was so unprepared.

"It's not possible," he said finally. "He had lifelines and pad-eyes all over the boat to hook onto. What about the life raft?"

"I don't know," Chaim said. "I don't even know the latitude and longitude. You want me to call the Coasties?"

"Yes. No. No, I'll have Barbara call them from here. Chaim. Thanks. I'll get back to you."

Roger hung up. He was staggered. Six months! The yard had worked six months, sometimes day and night, to transform *Hound of Ulster* from a plastic shell into one of the fastest, most responsive monohulls afloat. And the expense! The winches alone were worth more than some yachts. That they were still unpaid for was, from a practical standpoint, unfortunate. But what was utterly ruinous—and Roger's primary concern—was that his father, Spencer, in a rash and intuitive gesture, had insured the yacht at his own risk. If she were lost offshore, Spencer would be liable for part, perhaps all, of the yacht's insured value of $200,000.

"What's up?"

7

Griffen Monday, the rigger, had shut down the electric motor and secured the rigging boom. Roger could see by his expression that he'd heard most of the phone conversation.

"They sighted *Hound* this morning," Roger said. "She's a derelict. Con Macroth is missing."

When Roger told Barbara, her first thoughts were for Cath Macroth and her daughter Derdriu. Actually, Derdriu, twelve, would probably survive this emergency. For one thing she had Betsy, Barbara's eleven-year-old. Betsy was Derd's best friend. Cath, however, was another matter.

"She stinks in a crisis, Roger. There's no telling how she'll respond to this. I'd better walk over there before she hears it on the news."

Roger shook his head. "Not yet," he said. "All we know is the boat's floating around in the middle of the ocean. Maybe Con is too. Before we start spreading gloom and speculation, let's talk to Search and Rescue. Call Governor's Island and get all you can. I've got to finish this forestay by ten or the owner'll serve my head on a tray."

Roger left. The spring on the screen door made a nice, secure, summery sound. Barbara took a deep breath and picked up the phone. She was put through to Coast Guard Rescue Coordinating Center. Lieutenant Quinn answered.

"Just a moment, miss," said the lieutenant. "We have a hold on that."

The line clicked and she was shunted through several extensions. Finally, a friendly Texas voice came on.

"Ma'am? Thiz Lieutenant Harper in Documentation? We'gonna get you back to RCC in a minute. But first would you hep us?"

"I'll try," said Barbara.

"Thank you, ma'am. Here's the pro'lem. When Lieutenant Quinn filed *Hound of Ulster* with Documentation, the computer came up empty. We never heard of the boat. You say you commissioned her?"

"Yes."

"Okay." There was a click and the beep of a tape recorder. Lieutenant Harper cleared his throat.

"Is the yacht *Hound of Ulster* a U.S. or foreign flag vessel?"

"U.S." said Barbara. "At least she flew the U.S. ensign. The hull was built in Quebec but she was fitted out here in Sandwich."

"'Kay. Was she documented or numbered?"

Barbara froze. She always handled the documentation and numbering of new boats in the yard. But *Hound* had been so far behind schedule that no one had thought about it until she was already on her way to England.

"Gee, I don't know," she said, lying for the first time in her life to the United States Government. (It took her weeks to get over this. Later she bought two hundred dollars' worth of U.S. Savings Bonds and a silver Centennial medal from the Franklin Mint.)

"'Kay," said Lieutenant Harper. "Do you recall the name and address of the owner or owners?"

"Sure."

"Please state name and address of the owner or owners of the yacht *Hound of Ulster* believed to be of U.S. registry."

"Will do," Barbara said, easily intimidated into officialese. She opened her desk file. "The owner is ... the Macroth Corporation. They're urban-design consultants and contractors."

"Spell please."

"Macroth," she said. "Mike-Alpha-Charlie-Romeo-Oscar-Tango-Hotel. Do you read?"

"Affirmative," said the lieutenant.

"Address," said Barbara. "One-one-five Waterford Street. I spell: Whisky-Alpha-Tango-Echo-Romeo-Foxtrot-Oscar-Romeo-Delta Street in the city of New London, November-Echo-"

"Okay," interrupted Harper. "That's New London, Connecticut. You got a zip, ma'am?"

"Zero-six-three-two-zero."

"We could use you down here, ma'am," the lieutenant said sincerely. "Do you have a phone number for Macroth Corporation of 115 Waterford Street, New London, Connecticut 06320?"

Barbara gave it.

"And, ma'am, do you have the name of the yacht's captain?"

"Yes. It's Con Macroth."

"Request you spell first name."

"Charlie-Oscar-November."

"Con Macroth. U.S. citizen?"

Barbara hesitated. "Um ... I think Canadian. But originally from Ireland. Or England, maybe. I'm really not positive." She was telling the truth.

"And do you have a home address and phone for him?"

She had. But she didn't want them calling Cath. "I'm sorry," she said. "The company's all I have."

"'Kay, ma'am. One more question. To your knowledge, was Macroth a participant in the Observer Single-Handed Transatlantic Race which departed Plymouth, England, 5 June?"

"Yes."

Lieutenant Harper thanked her for the information, switched off the tape recorder and transferred her call back to the Rescue Coordinating Center. After a moment Lieutenant Quinn read her the Telex from CRCC Halifax.

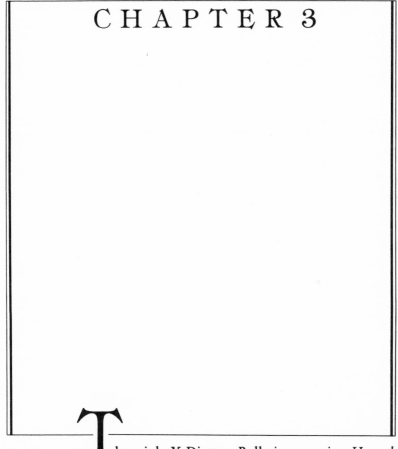

# CHAPTER 3

The triple-X Distress Bulletin reporting *Hound of Ulster* abandoned was also picked up in Newport, Rhode Island, and relayed to the Goat Island office of the Observer Single-Handed Race (OSTAR). In contrast to the general high spirits in town and the glorious spectacle of the OpSail tall ships jamming the harbor, the mood at OSTAR was grim. The race was already a disaster. Five boats sunk, dozens of dropouts and gear failures, Henderson forced back to Plymouth, Macauley unreported, Kramer presumed lost. And now Macroth.

Young Archer Leonetti, earringed, ponytailed and just a little spaced out, heard the news from one of the dockmasters at breakfast. Arch had been in Newport a week, stationed there by his uncle to boatsit *Hound* when she arrived. He finished his granola and honey and called his uncle in Meriden. The line was busy.

A tailor from J. Press was trying to take Marshall Leonetti's measurements. Leonetti stood in the middle of his office atop the Meriden Jai Alai building and talked into the long extension phone. What made it difficult for the tailor was that Leonetti walked when he talked. The tailor finally sat back on his heels and waited while Leonetti talked and walked and watched himself in the mirrored walls.

"Rudy, the lease is six thou a month for a restaurant operation of that size in my building next to my fronton. Casa Caserta pays seven downtown across from a Chevron station." He hung up and came back to the tailor. "I'm sorry," he said. "You've been very patient."

The tailor resumed his work. Marshall gazed into the mirrored wall before him. He enjoyed these seasonal visits from J. Press. Press had been his tailor for twenty years, since his days at Yale, and this small, exclusive ritual gave him a pleasant feeling of continuity. He smiled. The pale, still-boyish face with wide blue eyes set beneath curly red hair smiled back. "Wasp wop," he said aloud.

The tailor looked up from his kneeling position.

Marshall spoke to the mirror. "I don't want the trouser to break," he said. "Seersucker should be straight, don't you think? No flare. Not too Cardin."

The tailor from J. Press looked pained. "Cardin," he said, "is French."

The phone rang. The tailor stopped again. Marshall Leonetti walked to his desk. "Hi, Arch. How's Newport? My horse come in yet?"

Arch told him the news. In an impulsive and uncharacteristic gesture, Marshall Leonetti slammed the top of the desk with the palm of his hand.

"Shit!" he said. This was also uncharacteristic. He never swore and would permit no profanity among his employees.

"Well," he said finally, "that's a shock."

"Really."

12

"Where's the boat now?"

"Out there," his nephew replied. "She's a setup for salvage, Marsh. Like anybody could bring her in. I'd dig to bring her in if you'd go for it 'cause this town has me pigged out."

Marshall's face was impassive. "No," he said. "Come home."

He hung up, flipped through his addressograph and dialed the Macroth Corporation. Jane Pond, Con Macroth's secretary, answered.

"Yes, I've already heard," she said. "My brother called."

Marshall barely knew Jane Pond; only that she was one of those forever-Vassar girls who, fifteen years out of college, still wore a polo coat with pearl buttons and a barrette in her graying page boy.

"Your brother?"

"Roger Truly. His yard commissioned the boat."

Marshall didn't know him. "Is Desmond Macroth there?" he asked.

"No, sir."

"Has he heard?"

"I really don't know."

Marshall was getting annoyed. "Well, find him and have him call me immediately. And before you leave tonight send a couple dozen roses to Cath Macroth."

Jane hesitated. "Uh, don't you think that's a little premature?"

"No. Send them."

"Yes, Mr. Leonetti."

He decided Jane Pond had to go.

Roger Truly came back into the yard office, dumped the old PJ 43 wire forestay in a corner and peered over Barbara's shoulder. She had just finished typing the Halifax message. "I don't understand a word of this," she said, yanking the sheet out of the electric typewriter.

Roger smoothed the message on the top of the desk with a certain reverence. He read through it once, then translated for Barbara.

"St. John's Radio, call letters V-O-N, received a message from

13

the French motor vessel *Bearn,* call letters F-A-P-Z, at 1148 Zulu. Zulu is the same as Greenwich Mean Time. *Bearn* had attempted to salvage *Hound* three hundred fifty nautical miles east of St. John's in latitude 46–36 north, longitude 44–06 west. There was no one aboard. *Bearn* took off Con's logbook and some tape cassettes."

"What were the tapes for?" asked Barbara.

"He was planning a movie of the trip, I think; or maybe a book." Roger returned to the message. "*Bearn* took *Hound* in tow but had to drop it at 1130 Zulu because . . ." Roger read from the message. "'Unable tow speed required make ETA thirty June SPM.'"

"Gobble-gobble," said Barbara.

"*Bearn* couldn't tow *Hound* faster than seven knots. She probably needed to steam at fifteen to make her expected time of arrival in SPM. So she dropped the tow."

"What's SPM?"

"St. Pierre and Miquelon."

"Is that a place or a French law firm?"

"Two French islands . . . three actually . . . about fifteen miles off the south coast of Newfoundland."

Roger pulled an old chart of the North Atlantic out of his desk drawer. He unfolded it. The chart was covered with ancient coffee stains and bits of pipe tobacco from a long-ago adventure-planning session with Spencer. Roger located *Hound's* abandoned position and marked it with an X.

Barbara watched in silence. He seemed already at sea. "You're going after her, aren't you?" she asked quietly.

Roger put away the chart. "Yes," he said. "I'm going after her. I can't have my father in the slammer." He closed the desk drawer. "I think you should go over to Cath Macroth's house now. And, when you get back, order me an airplane ticket to St. Pierre for tomorrow. I want to talk to the skipper of that French vessel before I go stumbling off in the Grand Banks fog."

Barbara looked at the tall, rumpled figure which seemed permanently windblown. She stifled an impulse to smooth the dusty blond hair and the droopy mustache.

14

"All right," she said, picking up her purse. "I'm not exactly looking forward to this."

Roger patted her shoulder.

"What's that for?"

"Neat appearance," he said, not meeting her gaze.

She went out the side door and took the shortcut to Cath's.

Roger slumped in his desk chair and looked through the window at the jumble of sailboats in the basin. Coincidentally, the only empty slip in the basin was the one that had belonged to *Hound of Ulster*. Roger wondered if the anchor was still under the porch. . . .

# CHAPTER 4

The year before, in early fall, a man Roger had never seen came to the yard with an enormous CQR plow anchor in the back of his Land Rover. The man had a Scots accent which occasionally went Irish. His name was Con Macroth. He'd bought the anchor on sale in New Jersey and wanted Roger to store it for him until his new boat arrived. Roger put the CQR (big enough to hold a destroyer in a typhoon) under the office porch with the moorings and forgot about it.

Truly's Boatyard began hauling in late September and, for the extended insurance coverage skippers, continued into December. The fall was warm but wet. There was a late equinoctial gale on Halloween which threatened to run the Connecticut River over her banks and carry Sandwich into the Sound.

That morning, Roger, Griff Monday and Bryan Davidson, sweating in foul-weather gear, were fighting the winter cover on a Bermuda 40 in a gale of wind. The yard, under dirty, scudding stratus clouds, looked like no-man's land, the gravel gone to slimy mud and the potholes black and deep in rainwater. At the entrance to Truly's, as with most boatyards, there was an enormous crater in the road. Here the water was six inches deep and covered with whitecaps.

The red-and-white tractor trailer with Quebec plates snorted over the narrow service road, shifting down and belching black diesel out of its dirty chromed stack. At the yard gate the tractor plunged into the crater, sending a sea of solid water over the cab and onto the foredeck of the yacht on the flatbed trailer behind. The boat shuddered and rolled as the suicide trailer yawed through the great pothole. And then, with a final bellow and hissing of hydraulics, the rig jerked to a halt by the travel lift and Roger got his first look at *Hound of Ulster.*

She was a Rushton 39. Roger was not prepared for her. And he'd forgotten about Con Macroth who was now happily splashing toward him with the rain streaming off his black curly hair, a triumphant grin on his face. A month ago, when Con had dropped off the anchor and talked about a new boat, Roger had expected—if he'd expected anything—a Westsail or a Cheoy Lee . . . something big and heavy and slow. But the hull sitting on the trailer before him was another matter. Designed by Dick Rushton, one of the most innovative and creative young naval architects in the business, she was the last word in pure boat speed. From her swept fin keel to her high-aspect outboard rudder, from her crowned flush deck to her radically reversed transom, she was what Roger loved most in an ocean racing boat: light, strong and fast. But she wasn't finished.

Con, short on funds and hoping for a commercial sponsor, had been forced to go shopping for a builder. The lowest bidder, Carver Yachts of Ste. Marie, Quebec, had got the contract. For sixty thousand dollars they built a hull, keel, rudder, deck, house, cockpit and coamings. That's as far as the money went. There were no chain plates, winch pads, mast step or partner; no spars,

17

no rigging and, of course, no hardware. Though Roger didn't know it at that moment, he, Griff and Bryan would spend the next six months finishing the yacht against deadlines: deadline for the sail loft (Thanksgiving), deadline for sea trials (Christmas), deadline for offshore single-handed qualification trial (March) and deadline for departure for England (April). The final cost to Con would be four times the initial investment.

"Launch her now?" said Roger.

"Of course, man," said Macroth. " 'Tis Halloween. For a Celt, Halloween is the best possible time for a launching!"

Roger cranked up the travel lift. The wheels sank halfway to their hubs in the mud as the straps took the weight of the boat off the flatbed. However, like most of the village of Sandwich, Truly's sat on rock ledge and the huge airliner tires finally struck bottom. The travel lift inched the boat toward the water.

Roger directed the operation but Con Macroth was everywhere, checking the slings and lashings, sighting the wheel alignment along the tracks; obsessed, as if his life depended on the success of the launching. Drenched to the skin, his heavy Irish sweater hanging from his shoulders like a poorly fitting coat of mail, Con leaped onto the foredeck as the yacht's keel touched the water. Still supported by the slings and swaying slightly, the hull dropped lower until, finally, the straps went slack and she floated. Roger shut down the noisy travel lift and, for the first time in two days, the rain stopped. There was no sound except dripping. Con looked up at the crew on the dock and, with the utmost charm, whispered, "Sure, now we'll have a party."

And what a party it was! "Bee-zar," Barbara called it.

The Macroths owned a two-story Federal on Pleasant Street. That the house was less than a quarter mile from the boatyard was the principal reason Con had selected Truly's to do the work on Hound. The other reason was that his daughter, Derdriu, was friends with Betsy Foster, Barbara's girl.

No one knew the Macroths well. They'd been in Sandwich less than a year. But everyone knew about the Halloween party.

Sandwich was a yachty town. Topsider and Breton Red yachty: a little one-design racing, a little cruising downeast in July, maybe Block Island Week or the Vineyard Race; at the outside, the Newport-Bermuda. Yachty. No one from Sandwich had ever entered the OSTAR. Until now. People were curious. Dozens of citizens of normally well-behaved Sandwich crashed the party.

About eight P.M., Derdriu and Betsy, carrying their loot in shopping bags, returned from trick-or-treating and led Roger and Barbara over fences and backyards to the Macroth house. They needn't have bothered. Roger and Barbara could hear the party from the boatyard. The din was awesome. It sounded like a union meeting with a rehearsal studio next door. In the parlor, the FM radio played the Rolling Stones. In the living room, the eight-track stereo boomed out Brahms' Violin Concerto. Also in the living room was a two-manual electric organ back-to-back with a small upright piano. The organ had an outrageous electronic rhythm attachment which, at the press of a button, produced foxtrots, sambas, rhumbas or rock'n roll, complete with percussion. To Mick Jagger and Jascha Heifetz, then, were added "Chopsticks" and "Heart and Soul" played in every conceivable rhythm pattern. And, over this cacophony, voices had to be raised to be audible.

"Who's here?" shrieked a Blue Jay skipper.

"Everybody!" shouted a laser freak.

As is normal with children, Derdriu led Roger and Barbara into the house through the kitchen. A pale woman, wearing an apron over a brocade caftan, was filling a tray with hors d'oeuvres.

"Mummy, I have fourteen Twinkies," said Derdriu. "This is Betsy's mom . . . and Mr. Truly. May Betsy and I please have some wine?"

"Don't say 'mom,' darling. You're not American." She turned. "Hallo. I'm Cath Macroth."

She seemed remote and English. She didn't offer to shake hands but acknowledged them with the barest trace of a smile

19

and a fluttering glance. Roger thought the luminous face quite beautiful. But the short hair was brittle and almost white while the caftan betokened a lumpy lady beneath.

"There is a vast supply of spirits in the parlor," she said without enthusiasm, "as well as punch and mulled wine. Will you allow Betsy a glass of wine? I'm sure it's less harmful than your Twinkies."

Up yours, Barbara thought. They're not my Twinkies.

That Halloween night was the first time Roger had seen Con Macroth indoors. He seemed too big for the room; not in size—he was under six feet—but in intensity. Whether he was discussing the boat or mulling wine, he seemed huge and uncontainable. And diverse, Roger thought later as he stood in the parlor before a bookshelf displaying such motley titles as *Stress Analysis for the Mild Steel Truss, Lady Windermere's Fan, Bowditch's American Practical Navigator* and the *Peters Edition of Bach's Well-Tempered Clavier.*

A lot of people got sloshed at that party. The twenty-year-old tractor trailer driver from Quebec was the first casualty. He was put to bed in the guest room under the overcoats. About ten o'clock, without asking, Derdriu switched from mulled wine to beer. Roger happened to be near the scene of the demise. He and Con carried her upstairs, took off her shoes and put her to bed. Con had brought some implements with him. Roger now saw that these were fireplace tongs and a poker. With Derdriu tucked in and the light out, Con placed the tongs and poker on the floor at the foot of her bed. He placed them in the form of a cross.

"To protect the cradle from changelings," he said quietly.

A little before midnight, there was an almost imperceptible shift in the noise. The organ stopped and someone started playing the piano. Eventually the stereo was turned off; then the radio. The party moved into the living room and settled around the piano. Whoever was playing certainly had dexterity and style. Requests were filled. They ran the gamut from Cole Porter to James Taylor. Finally, at the stroke of midnight and without warning, the music stopped. There were groans from the guests.

"More! Encore!"

Con got up from the piano. He climbed onto the piano bench and picked up a pair of brass candlesticks. One was lit, the other not. It took him a moment to get silence.

"Quiet, please," he said. "Quiet, ladies and gentlemen." The murmuring died away. "The time has come to turn to more solemn matters," he said, "which will, I hope, bring luck and prosperity to all here.

"In ancient Ireland," he continued, "this night was called the Eve of Samahain. It marked the end of the grazing and the start of the Celtic New Year. It was the juncture of the old and the new; a night of dread and danger when ghosts and demons were abroad and the future could be seen; when the Druids discerned who would marry, thrive or die in the coming year."

Roger remembered he had stood only a few feet from Cath during this. He watched her as she watched Con. She seemed terrified. The glass in her hand trembled.

"At midnight on the Eve of Samahain," Con said, "all fires were put out and relighted." Symbolically, he lighted the unlit candle and blew out the other. The smoke from the extinguished wick rose to the ceiling. Roger could smell the hot wax.

"For a Celt," Con went on, "this day had great merit. 'Twas a fine day for drinking . . . "

(Laughter and a few "Yaaays.")

"A fine day for making love . . ."

(Spontaneous "Yaaays," a pause, a single "Boo," then laughter.)

"But, in particular, it was a fine day for the launching of a ship!"

Everyone cheered and clapped. Until the crash. Cath had thrown her wine glass against the fireplace. The room was stunned into silence.

"You bastard!" she gasped. "If you try to sail that stupid boat across the ocean, I'll never see you again!"

Roger wondered if the anchor was still under the porch. Through the office window, he watched a J24 ghost come into the basin and alongside the rigging dock. He realized he hadn't

21

called Spencer yet to tell him Con Macroth was missing and the boat adrift on the Grand Banks.

It was 9:45. He picked up the phone and dialed his father's office number.

# CHAPTER 5

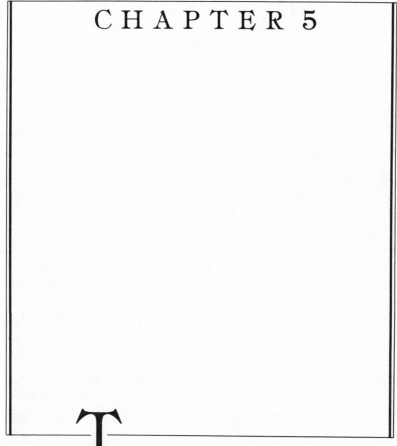

The letter carrier reached out of his red, white and blue Jeep and opened the Macroth mailbox. He tossed in a mail order catalogue and a phone bill.

"I'll take those, Mr. Narducci."

He turned and saw Barbara Foster. She stood on the sidewalk in a little patch of sunlight. Narducci, a supporter of Catholic College football, thought Barbara's hair, with the sun on it, looked like a Notre Dame helmet. With complete propriety and no feeling of disloyalty to his wife, he told Barbara he wished he were twenty years younger.

She giggled good-naturedly, took the mail and strode up the Macroth driveway with her long-legged walk. Barbara got her share of attention and admiration. At thirty-two, she had hips like a boy and a narrow waist that flared gracefully into the tapered torso and wide shoulders of a Domergue poster mannequin. The slender face was strong and tanned and the wide eyes Wisconsin blue with just the beginnings of twinkle lines at the corners ("Hummingbird's feet, Roger, not crow's feet"). And, to top it all off was the thick, straight, taffy-colored, infuriating hair; infuriating, that is, to other women. Barbara never had to set her hair or put it up at night. She just dried it and shook it and it fell into place. One older Sandwich woman, a sculptress who had known Henry James, said of Barbara, "We could never be friends. I can't be comfortable with her unless I wear a hat, and nobody wears hats anymore."

Barbara walked past the garage and let herself in through the back door. She was apprehensive. After their first chilly meeting, she and Cath had achieved a sort of punctilious friendship. But she had no real knowledge of the woman nor any idea how she would react to this news.

As she entered the kitchen her heart nearly stopped. An old man, wearing a tattered gray cardigan and floppy undershorts, was bent over a pot of boiling water on the stove. He wore a patch over one eye beneath steel-rimmed spectacles. His face was so close to the pot his glasses were opaque with steam. Barbara let out a little cry. He straightened and peered in her direction.

"Yes?" The voice sounded far away. The steamed spectacles suddenly cleared and she could see that the lens over the eye patch was window glass while the other was a thick, magnifying cataract lens. It made the old man look like a Cyclops.

"I am boiling an egg," he said, gazing at her with the one huge eye. "You'll be wanting Cath."

Barbara nodded.

"Off shopping," he said. "I am Damon Macroth, father of Conchobor the Intrepid." He turned back to the egg. "D'you know where her ladyship keeps the bloody spoon?" (He pronounced it "bludy spewn.") Barbara, her maternal instinct aroused, seated him at the kitchen table and made his breakfast.

Con's father was a talker. He lived alone and, like many of his kind, saved up things to talk about and didn't want to waste time listening. Of course, he loved nothing better than a new audience.

He was professor emeritus of Celtic literature at Queen's College, Belfast. He'd seen the start of the race in England and had come to the U.S. to see the finish. Not that he cared a damn for sailboats or England or the U.S. for that matter. But, with his wife dead these nine years, it filled the time and gave him respite from his crowning achievement, the *Compleat Unabridged Dictionary of the Gaelic Language*. He was almost blind and had to pamper his failing sight lest the lights go out for good before the work was completed.

He finished his tea. Then, with a note of scorn in his voice that surprised Barbara, he said, "In fact, her ladyship has announced we are to motor tomorrow to Newport, Rhode Island, to await the arrival of the *Hound of Ulster* with Magellan the Mick at the throttle." He shook his head. "*Hound of Ulster,* indeed! *Còin na Ulad.* Can you fancy the cheek of my own son? Him half a Yank and naming his millionaire boat after Ireland's greatest epic hero? The impertinence of the man!"

Barbara decided she shouldn't wait. She rinsed the egg and teacup and put them in the dishwasher. Then she sat across the table from the old man and told him his son was missing.

The eye blinked and stared at Barbara's mouth, where the words had come from. Finally, he coughed and turned away.

"Well," he said. "Well, he was always a bloody fool." The old man spoke again with a scornful, punitive tone. He gazed through the kitchen window at the bird feeder swarming with house finches. "A bloody fool! And callous! Insensitive! Selfish! Not a fundamental trace of consideration for others!" He took a deep breath. His voice shook. "He was taught the meaning of grandeur . . . and he chose gratification! Taught the meaning of nobility . . . and chose, instead, notoriety. He sent his mother to an early grave, did our boyo, and he'll do the same for the upperclass English bitch he's married to!" He raised a fist. "*Aided con Conchobor!*" he shouted in Gaelic.

He was silent, then, for a moment. He seemed out of breath. Finally he turned to Barbara.

25

"How long," he whispered, "can one survive in forty-five degree water? Fifteen minutes? Ten? They say it's not unpleasant, actually. A bit like nodding off in the dentist's chair. Sure, how would they know, never having drowned? Still, perhaps it is so. After the first panic, that is. Perhaps it is not unpleasant after the first, terrible panic when his hand misses the rail and clutches at the smooth sides of the yacht as it slides past and sails dutifully on. Soon it is but a wee dot on the horizon and he knows he is lost." The thin, purple lips curled back in a sneer. "Bloody, bloody fool!" All at once, the old man choked, stiffened and, with a howling intake of breath, began to sob. He shook his head in disbelief and the sobs burst out of him. He buried his face in his hands and the tears spurted between his fingers. Barbara got up and went to him. She tried to cradle his head against her but he pushed her away and kept her at arm's length. The thin shoulders shook in despair and the breath came in gasps. Barbara wanted to weep for the destructive old man who could neither give nor take comfort.

Minutes passed. Macroth eventually wrestled the sobs under control. He removed his spectacles, placed them on the kitchen table and wiped his face with a soiled handkerchief. He blew his nose.

"Most regretful," he said. "Self-indulgent." He sighed. "I've never had a drowned son."

There was a thumping at the front door. Barbara went into the hall and looked through the stained-glass vestibule window. Outside, in shades of blue, green and yellow, stood Cath, her arms filled with groceries.

"Somebody!" she sang out.

Barbara opened the door.

# CHAPTER 6

Spencer Truly was a gentle man who had managed to have a successful and happy life for sixty-seven years without doing any real harm to another soul. He had followed the strict tenets of Puritan piety and thrift set down by his Congregationalist preacher father but had tempered the stern paternal doctrine with humor, a certain amount of profanity and an early decision to do exactly as he pleased.

Spencer had taught Latin and history in several boys' schools. What little money he made, he saved. For some years before World War II, he conducted a camp for boys aboard a sixty-five foot schooner, cruising the Maine coast for two months each summer. There was little profit in it but, what there was, he cached. After the war, from which he emerged as a commander in the Coast Guard Reserve, he tired of teaching and went to work in various boatyards as a carpenter, joiner and rigger. He was finally hired by the owners of Sandwich Marine Service to run the yard at twice his schoolmaster's salary. He brought the old schooner to the main dock where he and his wife, Edie, lived aboard rent free. He spent little and saved much.

It was during this period, however, that Edie, who liked the academic life, presented Spencer with an ultimatum: he would have to choose between her and boats. Without malice, he chose boats and released Edie to the arms of an old bachelor friend and classmate who was headmaster of a school in Virginia.

After Roger bought the yard he moved aboard the schooner with his father. Spencer, now modestly wealthy, retired. From time to time he'd find a banged up boat, fix it and sell it at a profit. But it wasn't enough and he soon fell idle. Ultimately, he bought a small brokerage and insurance business a stone's throw from Truly's.

Spencer had built boats, surveyed boats and sold boats. But he had never insured boats. However, this didn't bother him. He had always relied on his seaman's eye and instinct. These two friends had never failed him.

When work started on Con Macroth's single-handed ocean racer, Spencer became as excited as Roger. He was at the yard every day. He even did some of the joiner work. As the yacht neared completion, the question of insurance arose. Macroth hadn't been able to get Aetna or Chubb or any of the usual marine insurance companies to underwrite a policy for the OSTAR. Lloyds of London would do it, but not for the full value of the vessel and at a premium that was forbidding.

Spencer, relying on his seaman's eye and instinct, as always, decided to gamble. He wrote Con a regular limited-navigation yacht policy for two hundred thousand with the Connecticut Provident Insurance Company. The policy covered *Hound of Ulster* from April 15 to November 15 between Eastport, Maine, and Brownsville, Texas. A rider was attached to extend the cruising area to St. John's, Newfoundland. Spencer then contacted an agent he knew in Southhampton, England, to write a policy covering the yacht for May and June while she was in English waters. Thus the boat was insured on both sides of the Atlantic but not in the middle. Spencer gambled that Con would make it through the middle. (Of course, nothing in either policy mentioned racing.)

When Roger walked into his father's office a half hour after he phoned, Spencer's sea bag was packed, his oilskins were stuffed into his boots and he was helping himself to a large scotch and water.

"Ah," said Roger. "Morning cocktails."

"I called Angus MacIvor in St. John's," Spencer said after a gulp. "He'll charter me his dragger *Stornoway* for six hundred fifty dollars a day. I've got to bring in that goddam sailboat, Roger, or I've bought the goddam farm."

Roger argued that it was pointless to go rushing off uninformed. "Wait," he said, "until we know which way she's drifting. Wait, at least, until I go to St. Pierre and get a deposition from the skipper of *Bearn*."

Spencer poured another. "I can't wait, for chrissakes! She could be run down. She could be pinched. She could be vandalized. That's my two hundred thousand goddam clams floating around out there. Anyway, Angus has radar and Loran and all those gizmos. You can always call me in St. John's if you learn anything from le capitaine of le froggy bateau."

In the end, Roger talked him out of going. The phone blinked on the desk. It was Barbara.

"How's Cath?" Roger asked.

"Weird. She seemed to resent the fact that I heard the news first. She went upstairs and took a bath."

"What about Derdriu?"

"Seems okay. She's with Betsy. Roger, the phone has really started ringing. The *New York Times* called. And *Soundings* and *Sail*. And Ernie Hall called. He said you'd talked to him about going after swordfish or mako."

"Yeah. Sometime."

"Well, he's chartered a Bertram out of Montauk Lake a week from Saturday. Do you want to go?"

"Tell him I'll let him know when I get back. What about my flight?"

"It takes two days. You're on Air Canada 682 out of Boston tomorrow afternoon. You change in Halifax for Sydney, Cape Breton, where you spend the night. Air St. Pierre has a flight from there to the islands at ten A.M. Fog permitting, you'll get in the same day as *Bearn*."

"Okay. One more thing. Wire the ship, care of St. Pierre, and tell them I'm coming. And make a reservation for me at any hotel."

There was a pause as she wrote down his instructions. "I guess that's all," she said finally. "Oh. If you have no exciting farewell-dinner plans, Derdriu and Betsy have made too much quahog chowder and it's going to be wonderful."

Desmond Macroth, Con's younger brother, was the last to hear. When Jane Pond called at eleven A.M., Des was making love to his latest mistress in her tiny studio apartment in Waterfield.

"Let it go," the girl whispered. "The machine'll answer it."

Des, already in the leafy suburbs of Nirvana, did not argue.

"Hi there," said the little-girl voice on the phone recorder. Des started to spasm. "This is Margie at 234-3658. I'm real sorry I'm not at home just now. But if you'll leave your name, number and message when you hear the lil' beep, I'll get back to you real soon. 'Bye and have a good one."

Afterward, Margie played back the tape. Jane said, "Urgent message for Des. Urgent." Des came out of the bathroom immaculate in linen slacks, bush jacket and silk foulard.

Desmond Macroth was Irish but thought of himself as English. This preference, which few Irishmen would acknowledge, was due, in part, to his striking resemblance to the actor Douglas Fairbanks, Jr. He was small, had Fairbanks's pleasantly aristocratic face, pale blue eyes and regimental mustache. He even used Yardley's pomade. Des was dapper (Con called him Desmond O'Dandy) and enormously popular with ladies over forty. Margie was twenty-eight. She'd never heard of Douglas Fairbanks but had seen one of his old swashbucklers on TV the night before she encountered Des at the restaurant where she worked. She asked him for his autograph. Des wrote on a cocktail napkin, "Alas, I fear I am not he/but fain will seek to mischief thee."

"Who rang, luv?" he asked.

"Jane Pond, from the office. She said it was urgent."

Des dialed. Jane told him what had happened and that he was to call Marshall Leonetti immediately.

"What's the matter, honey?" Margie asked when he put down the phone. "Was the call good news for Margie or bad news for Margie?"

Des picked up his briefcase.

"Dessy. Speak. Margie's not up for the silent treatment."

"I'll call you," he said perfunctorily, and went down the narrow stairs to his car. He unlocked the Camaro, got in and opened his briefcase. He took the cablegram out of the concealed compartment and read it again. It was from Harbour Grace, Newfoundland.

O'DANDY, DEAR. PASSAGE SALUTARY. BEST, DAVID.

# PART TWO

# *BEARN*

# CHAPTER 7

A dirty brown mist hung over Logan International Airport. Roger was early for his flight, having caught the Amtrak Pilgrim from New London. He sat in Air Canada's passenger lounge and went through a stack of material Chaim Gold had sent up by messenger from New York. There were satellite-facsimile weather maps of the east coast of North America for each day of the week ending the day *Hound* was sighted; current charts from Denmark Strait and the Labrador Sea to Cabot Strait and George's Bank; and the Pilot Charts of the North Atlantic Ocean for June and July. At the bottom of the stack, Chaim had included an article on the cuisine of St. Pierre-Miquelon clipped from an old *Gourmet* magazine. A note was appended: "After you locate the boat I want you to prepare yourself for the *Boeuf en Daube* at Chez Dutin as you would for your bar mitzvah. Only a pesky dose of clap prevents me from accompanying you on this glorious adventure."

Roger smiled. What a sweet, gentle, talented, funny friend, he thought. At college, Chaim had been Roger's savior, his catalyst and tonic. He'd awakened Roger's sensibilities and expectations and given him the gift of curiosity. And he taught him a little Yiddish. ("'Oi vay,' Roger, not 'Oh vay.' And loosen up. There is no such thing as lockjaw Yiddish.")

Roger kept out the July Pilot Chart and put the rest of the material in his sea bag.

He glanced at the chart. The glance, which took only a second, covered 120,000 square miles of ocean. Somewhere in that glance was *Hound of Ulster*. A tiny circle was penciled at latitude 47°N and longitude 44°–07'W, her last position. The trick to finding her would be in accurately predicting the direction of her drift since she was abandoned by *Bearn* thirty hours ago. Wind and current were the key ingredients.

The Pilot Chart, which showed average, not specific, conditions, indicated a thirty-two-percent probability of southwest winds at Force four (about fourteen knots) in the area 350 miles east of St. John's. Roger would later verify that probability against the actual weather map for 28 June (winds were, in fact, southwest at Force one to two).

He studied the current arrows. The Lab Current snaked its way down from the Labrador Sea, conforming to the contour of the land as far south as Cape Race, Newfoundland. A hundred miles offshore, the outer boundary of this icy ocean river met the Greenland Current and abruptly eddied east at about 0.8 knots. Further south, over the Grand Banks, the Gulf Stream caused another easterly eddy in the Lab Current. From her 1130 position yesterday, *Hound* was almost certainly drifting toward the east at about one nautical mile per hour. This area, northeast of the Flemish Cap, enjoyed twenty-five to thirty percent fog in July. And it was, Roger noted, a place where icebergs were not unknown. Finding the boat would be a pain. It would be an adventure in frustration and discomfort. It might be dangerous.

Roger recalled Spencer's blessing. "Be careful, for chrissake. I want that hooker back but not bad enough to hazard the health of my only begotten son."

*"Air Canada annonce le départ de leur Vol Six Cents Quatre-Vingt Deux pour Halifax. . . ."* The flight was announced in French and English. Roger felt butterflies. This feeling before a voyage had never gone away. Not since the first time when, as a child, he stood on the boat deck of the *Queen Mary* and quivered with delight as her great horn shattered the air above the North River, signaling departure. Roger picked up his sea bag and started toward the gate.

"Roj!"

He turned and saw his sister Jane running toward the lounge. Desmond Macroth trotted along behind her.

"Brought you a traveling companion," said Jane, out of breath.

Des looked pale and bewildered. His eyes were watery. Roger thought he'd been crying. But his "Hallo, old chap" reeked of dry martini and Certs. He excused himself and went to the men's room. Jane gave his ticket to the flight attendant and checked his bag.

"Des must be pretty shook up over this," said Roger. "Is he going to St. Pierre to represent Con?"

"I hope he won't be a problem, Roj. He's had a drop or two." She crossed her eyes. "Like a quart since breakfast."

Roger wanted to concentrate on the task ahead. He didn't know Con's brother very well and, though he realized it was uncharitable, the thought of having to be sympathetic and sociable for the next few days annoyed him.

Jane looked tired. She lowered her voice. "Very peculiar things going on at the office," she said. "This morning when I came in, Con's desk was locked. Never been locked before. Lot of the papers in the office safe have been transferred to the bank. Very peculiar. Other things too. However I don't wish to be disloyal." She forced a tremulous smile. "Well. I'm double parked. Have a good trip, dearie, and look after Des." She kissed her brother and loped across the reception area as if it were the varsity hockey field in greenest Poughkeepsie.

37

Roger realized Jane had driven Des to Logan all the way from New London, a prospect that would have terrified her before she went to work for Macroth Corporation a year ago. Roger had developed a new respect for his sister. She'd never done a day's work in her life. Never had to until her marriage to Gil Pond crashed. The divorce saved her from uselessness and gave her courage. But now she seemed frightened.

The DC-9 was half empty. Des took the window seat next to Roger. Turbulence over Massachusetts Bay kept the seat belt sign on. Finally they climbed out of the dingy altocum and into that eerie and radiant silence between the cloud top and the sky dome. The sign flashed off. Flight attendants began serving drinks.

Des settled into a straight-up Beefeater's and elaborately relaxed, as if he'd just turned the airplane's controls over to his copilot. If he was bereaved he didn't show it. He lit a cigarette and gazed at Roger.

"D'you know who the Hound of Ulster was?"

Roger put down the weather map he was reading.

"The Hound of Ulster," said Des, "was the Irish Ulysses. His name was Cúchulainn. He was the hero of the ancient Celtic epic, the *Taín Bó Cuailnge* which translates roughly as the 'Cattle Raid of Cooley.'" Des raised his glass and spoke in mock sepulchral. "Single-handed did Cúchulainn of Murtheimne defend Ulster against the warriors of Connacht who came to steal their cows and screw their women. He could slay eleven Connachtmen with one blow of his halberd, leaving the twelfth, the chap in the middle, unharmed. He could step on a lance in flight and stand upright on its point without piercing the soles of his feet." Des chug-a-lugged his drink. "He was a real jock, Roger."

Des asked the blonde flight attendant for another martini. Roger ordered a beer.

"Father taught Irish lit," continued Des. "Con and I had the Celtic sagas and epics, in Gaelic mind you, for breakfast, lunch and tea. They were; said father, the ancient pottage which savored the Irish temperament, gave it grandeur and nobility and without which there would have been no William Butler Yeats." Des chuckled. "Con swallowed the lot. He believed, or wanted to believe, every word of every tale. He wanted to believe that Cúchulainn, Hound of Ulster, could perform the salmon leap . . . a three-hundred-foot jump . . . or balance on the edge of a sword or, wearing his magic cloak, become invisible to his enemies. Con wanted to be Cúchulainn. And, of course, he wanted to please father."

The drinks came. Roger held them while Des paid the girl. After a sip, Roger said, "I guess most boys want to please their fathers."

Des snorted. "Not I, by a long shot! Father named Con after Conchobor, first King of Ulster. He named me after a steeple-chase jockey. Does that tell you anything? When I was born I expect he consulted the entrails of chickens and found the signs inauspicious." He shook his head. "And I doubt Con ever pleased father. The professor never gave approval; considered it a sign of weakness. But his lessons in grandeur took. With Con, that is. Not with me. I'm content with the safe, little life and an occasional martini. But Con scales the precipice! He walks the sword's edge! He never gives up."

Roger was silent. Why would a man whose brother was lost at sea talk such majestic nonsense?

"Con never gives up," Des repeated. "During the war, he and I were sent to Halifax to live with an aunt and uncle, safe from the blitz. Con was about ten. I was eight. When I returned to Belfast five years later, father got back the same little Desmond he'd sent off, only a bit older. But he got back a quite different Con.

"The uncle in Halifax was a professional musician. The aunt forced us to attend his piano concerts. My dear fellow, when I tell you I was paralyzed with boredom, I understate. But Con! My God, he was dazzled! By the sound, by the technical difficulty, by the applause and the uncle bowing. By the grandeur! Well. When it came time to return to Belfast, Con had abandoned Cúchulainn and decided to become Hector Berlioz. Father did not respond well to this metamorphosis. Particularly as Con

39

wanted to go back to the uncle in Halifax to study. Father sent him instead to Fife Ness School in Scotland."

Roger knew the school. It was a famous dungeon for bad boys on the east coast of Scotland. No central heating, wash in cold water by the dawn's early light, translate thirty lines of Cicero before breakfast. The regimen was supposed to build character.

"I don't see Con at Fife Ness," Roger said.

Des chuckled. "His stay there was not memorable. But he did learn one thing. He learnt to sail. The school had a fleet of dinghies and a few Dragons. In two months, Con sailed the lot. Then he stole one of the Dragons and headed for Halifax.

Roger was startled. "He sailed the North Atlantic in a Dragon?"

"No," said Des, finishing his drink. "But he got himself expelled, which was just as good. Eventually, he made his way back to Halifax and took his degree at Dalhousie with an organist named, I think, Schneider. You see, father was defeated in the end. Con never gives up."

"But after all that," said Roger, "why did Con become a builder of shopping centers and condominiums?"

Des seemed not to hear. He gazed through the perspex window at the tip of the wing suspended above the deep cloud cover. "Did you know," he said, "that, in ancient Ireland, Celtic warriors would try to stop a storm by rushing, fully armed, into the sea and slashing at the waves with their swords? Con is like that; not at all the sort of man who would be lost overboard."

Roger thought that was precisely the sort of man who would be lost overboard.

The airplane decelerated. The seat belt and no-smoking signs flashed on. Des waved his glass at the flight attendant. She was sorry but the aircraft was in its approach to Fax and no more drinks could be served.

Thus deprived, Des turned surly. He put on a pair of dark glasses.

"Of course," he said to Roger, "you and I are not here for the same reason, are we?" He smiled the drunk's strategic smile. "I

40

mean, I'm after the man, aren't I? While you're only after the boat."

The Fowler flaps deployed and the DC-9 jumped and slowed. They broke through the stratus and headed for final into Halifax.

"Actually, old boy," Des slurred, "why don't you fuck off? The bloody boat is worth more to us lost than found, if you'll pardon the touch of crass."

# CHAPTER 8

The defiance had seemed out of character for Des. Of the two Macroth brothers, he was the agreeable one who drank a little too much. Roger thought his outburst lacked conviction.

They switched airplanes in Halifax. By the time they reached Sydney, Cape Breton was in twilight and Des was in torpor. He passed out in the lobby of the Macleod Highland Hotel. Roger put him to bed and, next morning, fed him a vitamin-B and potassium cocktail (beef broth, V-8 juice, cabbage juice and three ounces of vodka). Des showed vital signs long enough to be put aboard the ten A.M. flight to St. Pierre.

With the exception of Halifax, most cities in Atlantic Canada are drab. Dictated by commercial necessity in a hostile environment, towns like Sydney and St. John's, Newfoundland, are dark brown fortresses built in a style variously known as Industrial Revolution Shanty or Early Bridgeport. For this reason, Roger was completely unprepared for the French islands of St. Pierre and Miquelon.

The Air St. Pierre Hawker-Siddley came in low over a suddenly fog-free, sparkling sea. To his right, during the glidepath, Roger caught a glimpse of needlerock reefs, cliffs and volcanic terrain which suddenly gave way to dockside cranes, cargo ships, a church and, as the airplane touched down, a half mountainside of shining, red-roofed houses painted in every imaginable color. The Hawker whined to a stop. Roger woke Des. After a few moments, the door was opened and they stepped into soft sunlight. Roger smelled seaweed, bread baking and Gauloise cigarrettes. A *gendarme* and *douhanier* stood in front of the tiny, lemon-yellow terminal. It wasn't Bridgeport. It was France.

The airfield was across a narrow strip of water from the town. Roger and Des cleared customs and hailed an old Citröen cab. They bumped away from the terminal, passed a small weather station and skirted Le Barachois, the inner harbor where dozens of deep-sheered, high-ended St. Pierre dories were drawn up on the shingle. The cab crossed the bustling Place du Général de Gaulle with its curious mixture of duty-free shops (filled, at the moment, with Japanese seamen), cafés, exchange-rate placards and pretty girls on motorbikes. Land-based pigeons, perched on the backs of park benches, gazed warily across the quay at seagulls, dressing the booms and tackles of deep-sea draggers like blossoms on a tulip tree.

Des suddenly stirred as a chic and deeply tanned young thing buzzed by on a scooter. The breeze, blowing her skirt, offered a glimpse of thigh. "Hallo," he said, "I think I'm better. Where are we?"

The Citröen stopped before a light blue building.

"Hotel Ile de France, messieurs."

They checked in. There were three messages waiting for Roger at the front desk. The first was from a Monsieur Foliot of the Bureau de Transport Maritime. M/V *Bearn* was at *le jetée*

Frigorifique. Captain Castaign would expect Monsieur Truly at 1400. The second message was from B. Chartier, Chef du Meteo, placing the SPM weather station at Roger's disposal as requested by Monsieur C. Gold of New York Meteo. Leave it to Chaim, thought Roger. The third was a cable from Barbara which said, simply, "Call tonight."

They had lunch at the hotel and walked to the docks. The Frigorifique pier was busy. Three ships were being worked. The vessel they sought was last in line. They approached her from astern. She was a former C-2 cargo vessel, old but clean. Her hull was black and there wasn't a spot of rust on her. Her booms were offloading cheese and Limoges china.

Roger gazed up at her counterstern, looming huge at the top of the tide. On her transom, in high-visibility orange, was painted "BEARN, Marseille." They climbed the steeply angled gangplank and were directed to the ship's small saloon.

Captain Castaign, in his early sixties, was a stocky, red-haired Breton gone gray who smoked incessantly. He was an old smoker and disdained filter tips. His lower lip was dotted with bits of cigarette paper from continuous daily contact with Gauloises Bleus. Two of his crew, Demonet and Lacombe, were present. Monsieur Foliot, of the Bureau de Transport Maritime, less than five feet tall, rotund and all business, would preside. As the meeting was to be conducted in French, an interpreter had been engaged. She was Mademoiselle deLille, a slim, tanned, multilingual St. Pierraise; the girl on the motor scooter.

As is the custom in France, everyone shook hands. There were murmurs of *plaisir* and *enchantez* while hands and arms crossed and recrossed the saloon table. During this casual Gallic ritual, Des became excessively British, holding each hand a bit too long and making certain he got the name. A steward brought bread, paté and wine.

M. Foliot called the meeting to order. Mademoiselle deLille put on a pair of enormous, tinted Saint Laurent glasses, opened a folder and prepared to read the depositions. The meeting almost ended before it started. Des had produced a tape recorder and clicked it on. Foliot rapped the table with his knuckles.

Mademoiselle translated. "M. Foliot had not the authority to permit an *appareil enregisteur* at an *assemblée reglementaire*. Monsieur will please surrender the machine until the meeting is terminated."

Mademoiselle slipped the glasses to the end of her nose and waited for Des's reaction. He smiled, turned to Foliot and asked him the one question no provincial bureaucrat wants to hear.

"If you don't have the authority, who has?"

Foliot didn't blink. *"Le chef du bureau à Paris."*

"Simply swell," said Des. "Let's ring him up."

Foliot leaned forward and fixed Des with a tiny stare.

"Sir," he said in English. Foliot, like many of his countrymen, spoke fluent English but preferred not to. To most Frenchmen, English is a form of pollution.

"Sir," he said, "it is seven P.M. in Paris. I would not presume to disturb the *chef du bureau* over a matter of so little importance to France. You take liberties, monsieur."

Des started to answer but Roger cut him short.

"Leave it," he said. "This meeting is a courtesy and no profit whatever to them. By holding it, they are simply obeying the international code of good marine manners. We're in no position to be fussy. Put the tape recorder away."

Des glared angrily at Roger. But the blue eyes seemed more amused than angry. For the second time, Roger had the impression Des was acting.

Roger turned to Foliot and, in his best NATO Navy French, apologized. For his associate the situation was most grave but this in no way diminished his esteem for the bureau, these gentlemen and mademoiselle. Let the meeting continue without interruption and without the *appareil enregisteur*.

Foliot nodded. Mademoiselle deLille replaced her glasses and began to read. Her voice was high and childlike.

"'On Monday, 28 June, in latitude 47–36 north, longitude 44–06 west, at approximately 0516 local time, M/V *Bearn*, G. Castaign, Master, perceived the sailing yacht *Hound of Ulster à babord* . . . to starboard . . . distance two hundred metre. A strobe light flash at the mast and his sail is partly up.'"

Roger took this to mean that *Hound* was reefed.

"'Wind is southwest at six knot; sea calm; some small fog. The yacht is called on VHF Radio Telephone channels sixteen, six, thirteen and also on low-frequency 2182 kHz. As there is no response, *Bearn* circle several time, stop to windward and speak the yacht by loud-hail microphone. As there is still no response, the hatch open and the cockpit empty, it is presumed either someone is injured or there is no one aboard.

"'M/V *Bearn* lay to and launch one of her boat. *Maître d'e-quippage* Demonet and *Marin* Lacombe . . .'"

"Hold on," said Des. "What's all that?"

"'Boatswain' and 'Seaman,'" said Roger.

Mademoiselle reddened slightly. *"Excusez-moi."*

"'Boatswain Demonet and Seaman Lacombe.

"'Boatswain Demonet and Seaman Lacombe row to the yacht and observe there is no one aboard. But everything below is in good order. The sail are neatly bagged, dish and cookware clean and stowed. The yacht *bouchains* . . .'" She looked at Roger.

"Bilges," he said.

"'The yacht bilges are dry. A sextant box is open on one of the berth. However, the sextant is missing (see separate deposition of Boatswain Demonet and Seaman Lacombe).'"

"Just a moment, mademoiselle." Des leaned forward. "The deposition states that the sextant box was open on the berth but the sextant was gone?"

Mademoiselle nodded.

Des turned to Captain Castaign. "Did you find the missing instrument anywhere else on the boat?"

The answer was negative.

Des leaned back from the table slowly. "Well," he sighed. "That's it, then, isn't it?" He looked at Roger. "At least now we know. He went over the side trying to take a sight."

No one spoke for a moment. Finally Foliot nodded to Mademoiselle deLille. *"Continuez."*

"'A search through the chart table show the chronometer in good working order. Also the radio receiver, tuned to CKZN, St. John's, is in good order. The yacht has no radio telephone.

"'Seaman Lacombe, an amateur photograph, take approximately fifty photo aboard the yacht. These photo are develop aboard *Bearn* and are appended to the deposition.

"'Boatswain Demonet find the logbook and several tape cassette which appear to have been made on the yacht. These are label "June 5–8, June 9–15, June 16–22 and June 23–blank." On the advice of *Bearn* owner, Société de Transport Maritime, these item are placed in a sack to be brought off the yacht before attempting salvage.

"'At 0610, Demonet and Lacombe fold the sail, put them below and close the hatch. The strobe light remain on and they return to *Bearn* with the sack containing the item mentioned.

"'M/V *Bearn* take *Hound of Ulster* in tow at 0632. But, by 0815, it become clear the yacht will not tow at a speed greater than eight knot. Consequently, as *Bearn* must honor her St. Pierre ETA of 30 June, which require a speed of fourteen knot, she abandon the yacht in fog at 0830, 1130 Zulu, Monday, 28 June in latitude 47–02.1 north, longitude 44–07.2 west.

"'Upon arrival in SPM, 30 June, the material taken from *Hound of Ulster* is placed in the custody of France (see appended statement by G. Foliot, Chef du BTM, Département de St. Pierre et Miquelon, France, Amérique du Nord).'

"The deposition is signed 'Gilbert Castaign, Commandant, M/V *Bearn*, S.T.M.'"

Mademoiselle deLille then went on to read the separate deposition of Boatswain Demonet and Seaman Lacombe. This was a more detailed account but added nothing to what had already been written. The statement by Foliot was simply a receipt, demanded by *Bearn*'s owners, absolving Captain Castaign and the company of any further responsibility.

"*Merci, mademoiselle,*" said Foliot. He turned to Roger. "*Messieurs, est-ce que vous avez des questions?*"

Roger asked Castaign if the emergency life raft was on the yacht when they boarded her. Castaign nodded.

"As monsieur will see in the photographs, the *canot pneumatic* was still in its canister with the holding straps fast to the deck."

47

So much for that. Des had no questions.

*"Bon,"* said Foliot. *"On va voir, maintenant, les fotos de Marin Lacombe."*

The photographs were brought out. Seaman Lacombe had done a thorough job for *Bearn's* fastidious owners. Everything had been photographed. To Roger, who had supervised the yard-work on *Hound,* it was like a family album.

There were shots of the bow pulpit, stemhead fitting, bow cleats and chocks, three views of the jib, shots of the forehatch, life lines, spinnaker poles, mast, spreaders and boom with reefed main up and under bare pole. There was a closeup of the un-opened four-man emergency life raft.

Lacombe had photographed everything on deck aft of the mast as well, from the turning blocks at the base of the stick to the stern pulpit, Aries vane gear and the overboard poles and horse-shoe rings (Roger had always wondered why a single-handed sailor would want this equipment as there would be no one to throw it to him if he went over).

Below, Lacombe had been no less thorough. He photographed the forepeak with bagged sails in bins, the chain plates, the head, Con's bunk, the chart table with Canadian chart 2666 spread open on it, the navigation rack, binocs, galley, dish stowage, the companion ladder with one of Con's safety harnesses hanging nearby, the quarter berths and the engineless engine bed under the cockpit sole where the canned goods were stowed. There were also photos of the radio, two tape recorders, the chrono-meter, the empty sextant box, the other safety harness and, lying next to a white canvas sack, the log book and four tape cassettes which were brought off by Demonet and Lacombe. Finally, there were several medium long shots of *Hound* taken from *Bearn's* boat. One had been taken while she was still under sail, before they boarded her.

Roger gazed at the carefully composed wide-angle photo-graph. She was ghosting along in light air under reefed main and working jib not fifty feet away. The photograph was filtered and misty, like a yachting portrait in the centerfold of *Soundings* magazine. But, beautifully composed as it was, there was something wrong with the picture.

During the captain's deposition, Roger had imagined himself on the bridge of *Bearn*. *Bearn*, heading west, had sighted the yacht to starboard. She had circled several times, stopped to windward of the yacht—that is, to the southwest of her—and put out a boat. Lacombe had, therefore, taken this photograph from the southwest. What bothered Roger was that the yacht was moving from left to right in the photograph. She was sailing east instead of west. She was not sailing, as she should have been, along the great circle course to Newport. He asked Lacombe if he had printed the picture backwards.

Lacombe pulled out his sheets of negatives. *"Non. C'est pas à la renverse."*

Castaign verified this. He had attributed the yacht's easterly course to variable currents and wind shifts. But Castaign, experienced as he was, was not a wind sailor and failed to realize that *Hound* could not have tacked or jibed herself without backing the jib and becoming hove-to. In the photo, the jib and main were on the same side; she was full and by on the starboard tack, heading east.

Roger knew that there were only two ways this could have happened. One was that, a week or more ago, *Hound* was heading *west* with the wind over her starboard quarter out of the northeast. Some time after Con was lost, the wind slowly backed 180 degrees into the southwest. The yacht, obeying the wind vane, went around the shift and headed east on the same tack. A check through Chaim's weather maps would probably show if a shift of that magnitude had occurred. The only other explanation for *Hound* heading east on starboard was that Con, finding himself too far to the north or too close to Newfoundland to the west, purposely tacked. That is, the boat was on starboard when he fell overboard.

"Really, Roger," interrupted Des. "What possible difference could it make? I mean, it's done. Who cares?"

Roger decided to drop it.

Captain Castaign cleared his throat and looked at his watch. *"Foliot, si je peut terminé."* Castaign leaned back. As always, he spoke with a cigarette in the corner of his mouth.

*"De mon avis, Macroth avait aucune raison de quitter le yacht . . ."* His deep glottal delivery contrasted with Mademoiselle deLille's flutelike translation.

"In my opinion, Macroth had no reason to abandon the yacht . . . at least no seaman's reason. The last wind and sea in that area was 18 June and that only Force six. The yacht was dry, there was no damage, no chafe, he was like new. The weather had been calm for ten days or the sextant box would not have remained on the berth nor the chart on the chart table.

"One could speculate that, during the night, Macroth struck an iceberg and was knocked overboard. It is doubtful. The only marks on the vessel are salt streaks. Of course, the missing sextant suggests that he went on deck to take a sight and lost his balance. It is possible. But, again, there is no proof. It is also possible he went over the side deliberately."

Des, who was still leafing through the photographs, looked at Castaign with interest. "Deliberately?" he said quietly. "With a sextant 'round his neck?"

"He may have had enough," said Castaign. "From my own knowledge I know it was a very difficult passage for your brother. We, In *Bearn* of eight thousand ton, had to heave-to during the gale of 14 June. For a man alone in a small yacht, at sea for three weeks, half of it in full gale . . ." He shrugged. "One had to be very strong. Fatigue, exhaustion . . ." He left the sentence unfinished and turned to Roger.

"The sea around the Flemish Cap is very unpredictable. If you intend to locate the yacht, do not rely entirely on the Pilot Chart for your set and drift. I would say he will drift more south than east. In any case, out there is fog and you will not find him in the fog; not until the stationary front has moved. And, in these latitudes, when the fog is gone it is not gone for long. You must act quickly. Your best friend, monsieur, is the Meteo. And your second best friend is the Coast Guard aeroplane."

The captain stood up followed by Foliot and the rest. The

meeting was over. Everyone shook hands again. Roger thanked Castaign, Demonet and Lacombe. Mademoiselle deLille put the depositions and photographs back in their folders and gave them to Des. "My condolences, monsieur," she said simply, and left before Des could reply.

Des put the folders on the saloon table and walked over to Foliot. Still annoyed over the tape-recorder incident, he sharply requested the sack containing Con's logbook and tapes. Foliot closed his eyes and placed his little hands flat on the table. The tapes and logbook would not be released before fifteen days.

Des was startled. "Fifteen days?"

"They will remain in bureau custody until my reports are filed and a release from Paris obtained."

Des was silent. Foliot opened his eyes and waited for the explosion. None came. Instead, Des smiled amiably, nodded and, without another word, walked out, leaving the folders on the table.

Roger thanked Foliot for all he'd done. Foliot explained that when Paris released the material taken from *Hound of Ulster*, it would be sent to Captain Macroth's next of kin. Could Roger supply the name and address of the next of kin? Roger gave him Cath's name and address.

Foliot then presented Roger a bill for $234.07 to compensate the owners of *Bearn* for lost time, for Lacombe's film and processing and for Mlle. deLille's services. Roger gave Foliot his personal check and got a receipt. They shook hands. Foliot offered to give him a lift. Roger declined, preferring to walk. He took the folders from the table, opened the heavy saloon door and stepped over the bulkhead into the whitest, most opaque fog he'd ever seen.

# CHAPTER 9

**D**es had groped his way to the ship's rail and walked aft to the gangplank. It was after five P.M. The ship was quiet. Cargo booms and slings were secured. The only sounds were of moving water between the pier pilings, an occasional gull's cry, and, from across Le Barachois, a deep foghorn sounding two blasts at intervals. The tide had dropped and the gangplank was nearly level.

Des went ashore and heard his footsteps echo along the Frigorifique. He realized he'd forgotten the folders. No use stumbling back aboard in this fog. If Roger didn't bring them, he'd go back to the ship tomorrow. He followed the halos of the pier lights until he came to the Quai à Charbon Road which led to the center of town. The fog was nearly impenetrable but, by keeping the sound of the foghorn in front of him and the white-washed curb to his left, he found he could make progress.

Des was immensely relieved. Things had worked out better than he'd any right to expect. The cold facts of the depositions, the unused life raft and empty sextant box would certainly satisfy Marshall Leonetti that Con had met with an accident. Anything to the contrary that might turn up in Con's log or the tapes would be safely tucked away in Foliot's office for two weeks or more. That was a bit of luck! In two weeks Leonetti would be so busy with the Shinecossett Recreation Facility, he wouldn't be interested in further details of this fiasco.

"Monsieur?"

The child's voice came from the right.

Des crossed the road and nearly bumped into the figure beside the motor scooter. It was Mademoiselle deLille.

"Ah," said Des with enthusiasm. "Is mademoiselle, dear, *en panne?*"

Mademoiselle smiled a full-mouthed smile showing small, perfect teeth.

"Monsieur Macroth," she piped, "I pray you can drive a vélo. I am blind in the fog."

"What sort of bike is it?" asked Des.

*"Un Kawasaki."*

Des got aboard and kicked the thing to life. Mademoiselle climbed on behind him and put her arms around his waist. To the iodine smell of low tide and the faintly acrid odor of the Kawasaki's exhaust was added the warm and close scent of Arpège. It was an exotic mélange. Des forgot about Marshall Leonetti.


Roger, remembering Chaim's counsel, phoned Chez Dutin for a dinner reservation. As it was booked solid, he ate in the hotel dining room. Roger and Des had been assigned the first sitting. Their table rested on chromed steel legs and was covered with a green oilcloth. It seated four. Des's chair was empty and Roger's dinner companions were two young French-Canadian nuns from Quebec City who had come to St. Pierre for a fortnight to study

French. This seemed redundant to Roger until he tried to understand their Québecois dialect.

Contrary to the dining-room decor, the food was excellent. Roger and the nuns giggled through two carafes of *vin ordinaire*. He excused himself before dessert and walked down the Rue Mâitre Georges Lefèvre to *téléphone centrale* in the Customs House. He placed a collect call to Barbara. The man at the operator's desk assigned him booth number 3. The call went through in less than a minute. Betsy answered and accepted the charges.

"Gads! It's about time! Mom wouldn't let me use the phone 'til you called. Guess what?"

"What?"

"They found Mr. Macroth."

Roger felt the blood drain from his face.

"Jesus! Where?"

"On television."

"No, dummy. Where on the ocean? Betsy, let me speak to your mother."

Roger's pulse was hammering. Barbara came on.

"It was on Channel Three news," she said. "The Russians picked up a man in a life raft at 1630 local time. Channel Three guessed it was Con."

"In a life raft?"

"Yes."

"Where?"

"Didn't say. Up there, I guess."

Roger was silent. It was impossible. Barbara could hear him thinking.

"Roger," she said quietly, "I know it's a big ocean, but this is all Cath and Derdriu have at the moment."

"Then don't tell them Con's life raft is still in its box on deck." He told her about the meeting on *Bearn*, about the depositions and photographs. "The photographs," he said, "have shaken me out of my armchair, Barbara. He's really dead."

"Well, I'm opting for divine intervention or a lady dolphin or something. I don't like sad endings. Speaking of that, your sister called. She's been fired."

"Jane? Fired from Macroth? Why?"

"They said she was 'overqualified.'"

"Who's 'they'?" he asked.

Barbara turned away from the phone. "Betsy, go sulk somewhere for a couple of minutes. And don't eavesdrop."

Roger heard Betsy groan and leave the room. Barbara came back on.

"Have you ever heard of Marshall Leonetti?"

Roger hadn't.

"Well, your sister has been quietly sitting on the most scandalous tangle of worms, if you'll excuse the tangled metaphor. I'm surprised she doesn't have an ulcer. Listen to this. Last March, before Con went on his qualification trial, he thought he had a sponsor. The sponsor was your favorite eatery: McDonald's. The plan was to sew the McDonald's logo on the mainsail and call the boat *Big Mac*. Con ordered a lot of last-minute stuff, signed for it and then the deal fell through. He was completely broke. He owed us, he owed the sail loft, the riggers, everybody. Jane said he was in the hole for seventy-five thousand without a prayer of paying. The banks wouldn't touch him, he already had a second mortgage on the house and Cath was insisting he sell the boat and forget the race. Enter Marshall Leonetti with a hundred thousand dollars."

"Who is Marshall Leonetti and where does he get that kind of cash?"

"I asked Jane the same question," said Barbara, "and all she said was 'Ahem.' Apparently he owns trucks, buys and sells construction companies and has something to do with Jai Alai."

"Sounds impeccably connected," Roger said. "What did Leonetti get from Con in return for his largesse?"

"Leonetti got the boat, he became a director on the board of Macroth with stock options and—this is my favorite—he gets one-third of Con's life insurance."

Roger whistled. "How much is Con's life insurance?"

55

"I don't know."

"Is Cath in on this?"

"I don't know."

"Des?"

"I don't know."

The phone clicked and the operator of *téléphone centrale* cut in. "Monsieur, *je m'éxcuse mais les salles de téléphone ferment à huits heures. Signalez quand vous aurez finis.*"

It was two minutes to eight.

"Dammit," Roger said. "We won't have time to talk about this. They're turning off the phones. How's Spencer?"

"He proposed to Betsy this morning. They're getting married as soon as Bets finishes the sixth grade."

"Sounds right. Tell them I'll bring a wedding present from St. Pierre. Barbara, when the fog lifts I'll go to St. John's. Contact Angus and tell him to have *Stornoway* ready the minute it clears."

"Okay."

Roger almost said "I miss you." Instead he said, "Good night and thanks for everything."

Barbara said "I miss you" and hung up.

Roger walked down the stairs and out into the fog. He skirted the flowerbeds in the Place du Général de Gaulle, crossed the square and made his way back to the hotel. The bar was in full swing. He stopped at the open door and, through the smoke inside which was almost as opaque as the fog outside, saw Des sitting with Mademoiselle deLille and a tableful of Japanese. Des, who had several empty glasses in front of him, spotted Roger and waved him over.

"The darling girl speaks seven languages, including Japanese," said Des weakly. "How about a drink?"

Roger declined. For the moment, he decided to give Des a wider berth.

"I had hoped," slurred Des, "that I could divert mademoiselle upstairs. It was a premature wish."

Roger went to his room and undressed. He had left the depositions and photos in their folders on the bureau. He went

56

through them once more, not fully concentrating. Des stumbled in next door. From the sounds through the wallboard, Roger guessed that Des had not scored with mademoiselle. He heard him fall into bed.

Roger brushed his teeth, turned out the light and climbed into bed. Des was snoring. The foghorn boomed in the distance. Another horn, higher and less powerful, bleated nearby; probably a breakwater horn. Roger dozed. He thought he couldn't have been completely asleep during the dream because his leg muscles twitched. But the dream was very clear. The UPS truck delivered the package in front of the boatyard office. Barbara signed for it. She was wearing a sundress and eating an ice-cream cone.

"It's Con's RDF," she said, smiling.

Roger sat up in bed and looked at his watch. It was two A.M. He'd been asleep for nearly three hours. He turned on the light. It took him a moment to realize where he was. Then he thought about Con's RDF.

Con had bought a pistol-grip radio direction finder called a "Seapoint" from a Boston firm that was about to go out of business. It ran on four AAA nonmagnetic, self-contained batteries and it had its own hand-bearing compass on top. It was a good unit except, for some unexplainable reason, the bulkhead mounting bracket was made of magnetic material and had to be discarded. Spencer built a new bracket for Con out of some teak scrap and a piece of shock cord. He mounted it on the bulkhead, forward of the chart table.

Roger, his curiosity aroused, went to the bureau and pulled out the photographs again. He found the one he was looking for. It showed the corner of the chart table, the bulkhead, the rack with Con's plotter and dividers and, above that, faintly, the RDF bracket that Spencer had made. Roger hadn't noticed before. The RDF was gone.

# CHAPTER 10

Truly's Boatyard and all of southeastern Connecticut was baking in ninety-degree heat.

"It's the goddam Bermuda High," said Spencer. "Son of a bitch is camped right on top of us. There won't be a decent sailing breeze around here for a month."

Some desultory explosions came from the supermarket parking lot where young boys with illegal firecrackers were prematurely celebrating the Fourth of July.

Barbara had deposited Betsy at Cath's. Derdriu was riding in a children's horse show and Cath took Betsy along to act as gofer. Actually Cath had planned to stay home. But when she got the news that the man in the raft was a merchant seaman who'd been picked up near the Azores, she packed the kids into the car and took off. Barbara looked forward to a relatively carefree Saturday at the yard.

She put a call through to Angus MacIvor on *Stornoway,* Job's Wharf, St. John's. While she was waiting for the operator to call back, Spencer came into the office to scrounge a cup of coffee and get his day started. Spencer was freshly shaved and bay rummed. He had a small earring of shaving cream under each lobe. Barbara adored him. He sat on the edge of her desk with his coffee and looked at her sideways. She knew what was coming. This was Spencer's when-the-hell-are-you-and-Roger-going-to-get-together look.

"When the hell are you and Roger going to get together?" he asked.

Barbara giggled. "I'm off Roger," she said. "I got the hots for Mikhail Baryshnikov.

"Who's he?"

"A welder at Electric Boat."

Spencer had asked Barbara this same question since she'd been at Truly's. Actually, the question was Spencer's way of apologizing to her for his son's inability to assign his affection. Roger was still gun-shy. Barbara had recovered from her failed marriage; Roger hadn't from his. That they had a sweet, warm and kindred affection for each other was plain. But it was a standoff.

The operator called back. She had Angus on the line. Barbara told him Roger was in St. Pierre, waiting to charter *Stornoway* for a square search.

"Lord Jaysus, Barbara," said Angus in his south-coast Newfoundland accent, "we're dat t'ick 'o fog it would be wunnerful if we could see t'bow of t'dragger."

There was no expectation of clearing weather for a week. He would not wish to go out of harbor to pick up a seine buoy, and that with a radar reflector on it, never mind making a search for a yacht over thousands of square miles of ocean. Spencer got on the phone. He and Angus discussed alternatives. With the visibility down to fifty yards, there appeared to be none but to wait.

"Roger might as well come home," Spencer said after he hung up. "Unless he's found himself a *jolie* mademoiselle to keep his butt warm in the fog."

"Fog you," said Barbara sweetly.

As all flights had been canceled, Des left St. Pierre on the morning ferry to Fortune Bay. He woke Roger at six, picked up the folders and with a cheery "Toodleoo old chap" disappeared. Roger didn't see him again for several weeks.

Roger visited Monsieur Chartier at the Meteo. He was most hospitable. He gave Roger the grand tour of the tiny weather station and supplied him with facsimile tear sheets, dewpoint and windspeed/direction data and barograph readings. It meant little. The wind northeast of the Flemish Cap, where *Hound* was drifting, was weak and variable. Fog extended from Labrador to Massachusetts. Chartier speculated that a weak cold front might improve things a bit in three or four days. Then again it might not. He remembered July of '64, in conditions much the same as these, when *la brume* had remained for one month.

Roger, in spite of urging to the contrary, stayed in St. Pierre for three more days. The reason he stayed was not because of the superb food at Chez Dutin and Le Caveau or because of a jolie mademoiselle. It was because he was a sailor and sailors are superstitious.

There are some things a sailor does not allow himself to do. He does not, for instance, if he's in passage, mention his destination aloud or, God forbid, write it in the log. To do so would immediately bring the wind on the nose. A sailor never shakes his fist or speaks crossly to the sea or sky as it could bring a gale or, worse, a flat calm. Some sailors do not allow whistling aboard. Others think it brings wind. Some sailors forbid pissing over the side for fear it will raise a gale. Others insist it is the only way to bring wind but specify which side, port or starboard, depending on the favored tack. Sailors, of course, do not trust the weather. And all the modern meteorological equipment in the world will not make a sailor trust the weatherman, Chaim notwithstanding. Roger was perfectly sure that, in spite of the satellite photos, the facsimiles and the fact that he could not see across the Place du Général de Gaulle, the fog would lift the minute he left St. Pierre.

Normally, the cargo vessel *Ile de St. Pierre* departs Le Barachois every Monday for the eighteen-hour trip across the Cabot Strait to Sydney. Her departure had been delayed until Wednesday. Roger booked passage.

During his last night at the hotel, he got up every two hours and looked out the window to see if the fog was still there. It was. It was there Wednesday morning when he went shopping and bought St. Pierre T-shirts for Derdriu and Betsy, a Jeantet pipe for Spencer and a yellow sundress from Paris for Barbara. It was there when the *Ile de St. Pierre* cast off her lines and, radar twirling, picked her way out of the *Passe de Nord* and around *Les Canailles* to the open sea. It was there, thick and motionless, in Sydney harbor the next day. There was even a little fog when Barbara met Roger at Logan Airport. And the first words out of her mouth were, "The Coast Guard reports *Hound* was sighted by an Argus aircraft from Gander."

"When?" asked Roger.

"The day you left St. Pierre."

# CHAPTER 11

And the day Roger left St. Pierre Spencer received a letter on Macroth Corporation stationery. The letter was Re: Connecticut Provident Insurance Co. Policy No. YA-16-23. It referred to a specific paragraph of the General Conditions of the policy and declared it would serve as official notice of the loss of the insured yacht *Hound of Ulster* in the Atlantic Ocean and the presumed death of the assured, Conchobor Macroth. In addition, it would serve as a claim on behalf of the agents for the assured for full benefits under the policy as provided in Sections et cetera et cetera. The letter was signed "Marshall V. Leonetti" with copies to Desmond J. Macroth and Douglas Adrian, Claims Dept., Connecticut Provident Insurance Co.

Spencer was amused that the "Official Notice" of the loss of the yacht arrived the day after she'd been sighted by the Cana-

dians. Nevertheless, he got a call Thursday afternoon from Doug
Adrian at Connecticut Provident inviting him to lunch in Hartford the next day.

"I've been summoned," Spencer told Barbara. He wasn't at the
yard when Roger got back on Friday. Roger and Barbara sat on
the office steps in the sunshine. Roger went through his mail. He
fussed. He worried about Spencer's meeting in Hartford. He
worried about the chances of another aircraft finding the yacht
and about the practicability of parachuting into the sea with a
life raft. He wondered if he shouldn't be in Gander. There were
no details from Canadian Rescue Center on the sighting. But
there were new coordinates which placed the yacht one hundred
miles south of her last position. Castaign had been right.

The immediacy of the sighting pushed the St. Pierre discov-
eries to one side. Con's missing sextant and RDF, that *Hound*
was sailing east instead of west when spotted by *Bearn*, that Marshall Leonetti was involved, all paled in importance beside the
physical fact that an Argus had sighted the yacht and come up
with a new position.

"You can't do anything," Barbara said. "Not right now. The
airplane found a hole. The fog is still there, thick as ever." Roger
tossed pieces of gravel. "You might as well go fishing."

"Why the hell would I want to go fishing?"

"Ernie Hall invited you."

Roger had forgotten. Ernie was going offshore tomorrow for
swordfish or mako and had asked him along. It seemed a frivo-
lous thing to do. Roger wanted to see Spencer and felt he ought
to visit Cath. And, of course, he didn't trust the weather. What
if the fog suddenly lifted on the Grand Banks while he was
hooked into a two-hundred-pound fish? He decided to call
Chaim.

"For a man who vilifies the science of meteorology the way
you do, you are a persistent caller," Chaim said. "Let me get my
crystal ball." He was back in a moment. "Okay. There's a weak
low traveling up the Gulf of Maine that won't pack enough air
to muss a tart's hair. Probably bring in an easterly flow that'll
intensify the fog. There's a fairly respectable Canadian high due

about, oh, Wednesday of next week which, if it doesn't stall, occlude or otherwise become a pain in the ass, might just do the trick with northwest winds Force five to seven. By the way, I expect a full report on your trip at some later date. Right now I'm busy with a forecast for the President's weekend golf at Pebble Beach. Tell Barbara my lips are swollen with desire for her. 'Bye."

Roger decided to go fishing. It would take his mind off the boat. He called Ernie at the Deep Sea Club in Montauk Lake.

"Terrific! Meet me at Oscar's," said Ernie. "Six-thirty."

Roger hadn't unpacked yet. He transferred his seabag from Barbara's car to his.

"I'll be back Sunday," he said. Then he remembered the presents he brought from St. Pierre. "The T-shirts are for the girls, the pipe's for Spencer and this is for you. I hope it fits."

As he drove out of the yard, he could see Barbara in his rearview mirror, holding the packages and gazing after him.

"Clod," he said aloud, as she faded from view. "Oaf and lout," he said. When he treated her so peremptorily it was some relief from the guilt he felt to call himself clownish names. It trivialized the anguish. Roger's fears would have been a simple matter for a psychotherapist. But he had been raised with the stupid Wasp dictum that there was nothing wrong with anyone that couldn't be cured by a few sets of tennis or a spinnaker reach in thirty knots of wind.

He turned onto Interstate 95 and headed for New London and the Orient Point Ferry. He felt foolish and angry and realized he was thinking about Katya.

During his last year in the Navy he'd been made an assistant U.S. Naval Attaché in Brussels. There, at a consulate party, he met Katya Alexandrova, a Kirov dancer who'd defected to the West when the company performed in Antwerp. She was two years older than Roger and not a particularly good dancer. But she dazzled him with a sort of sinuous, exotic charm, an outrageous sense of humor and what Roger perceived to be the perfect body. No one was deceived by Katya's interest in the young naval lieutenant. She wanted a ticket to New York. But Roger, young and foolish, didn't care. He'd never met anyone like Katya and he felt if he didn't seize this opportunity to obtain his private Terpsichore he would never forgive himself.

The marriage lasted about an hour and a half, or until he got out of the Navy and they landed in New York. Katya responded to Western freedom in a most un-Soviet way. She hung up her ballet shoes forever and flung her perfect pelvis at a Gulf and Western executive who had a wife, three children, a house in Great Neck and an income of around a half a million a year. The last time Roger saw her, she was slithering out of their West Village apartment, newly Blackglama'd and Tiffany'd (downpayments from the Great Necker).

"Trushka," she said—she never called him "Roger"—"you are sweet but too poor, too provincial and you are lousy *yopt*. *Yopt* is like ballet, darling: you must learn technique before you can perform."

Roger was destroyed. Chaim came to his rescue. He saw that his friend had been effectively castrated. It was simplistic and rudimentary. A more sophisticated man would have understood Katya's parting shot as the mean, self-justifying tactic of a bitchy adventuress. Not Roger. Chaim tried counsel. It failed. He tried humor. He even made Roger a Sex Kit.

"Place Right Hand A on Breast B and slowly manipulate Nipple C. Place pre-inflated Member D (see note for inflation procedure) into Prepared Orifice E (see preparation note). . . ."

Roger laughed but it didn't help.

"Get a book!" cried Chaim. "Read some porno! Learn from the experts!" But then he sat Roger down and spoke seriously. "I don't think you've been in love yet," he said. "If you think of sex as 'performing' then you're standing outside yourself and watching. Isn't that the word she used? 'Performing'?" In the end, Chaim made a joke. It was all he could do.

"Anyway, I'll wager one lady's poison is another lady's meat," he said. "Pun intended."

Roger caught the ferry to Orient Point and arrived at Oscar's a half hour before Ernie.

Oscar's was a fishermen's bar with a dozen tables. It was in the village just off the old Montauk Highway. Inside the front door was a sign that said "Oscar's name is Tony." Tony's wife was the cook. Each night she made one magnificent dish. When there was fresh fish it was fresh fish. Otherwise it was *scungili, zuppa de pesca,* clams *oreganato* or *possilipe* or *muscoli* linguine.

Roger took a table, ordered a drink and looked around him. No attempt had been made at decoration. None was needed. At the back of the bar, over the bottles and the blue mirror, was a stuffed sailfish which Tony had caught in Florida years before. Everywhere else, the walls were covered with calling cards and postcards from friends and patrons on long-ago vacations, placards, humorous signs, cartoons, bits of pot warp, tattered fishing flags and markers, and photographs by the hundreds. Photographs of fish, men standing beside fish, men holding fish, fish being weighed, fish laid out on the dock. And boats. Egg Harbors, Bertrams, Pacemakers, Hatterases and Rybevitches with tuna towers and outriggers and fighting chairs. And older boats: Wheeler Playmates, Matthews, Richardsons and Elcos. And deep-sheered lobster boats, a few draggers, skiffs, catboats and a schooner or two. The bar was a museum and art gallery commemorating thirty years of sportfishing on eastern Long Island.

Ernie arrived. He was well known and well liked. Tony came over. So did others. Everyone bought a round or two. By the time the swordfish arrived Roger was feeling no pain and Tony was oiled.

"He's an authentic, functioning alcoholic," said Ernie. "If he stops drinking he'll get sick and die."

Roger finished his swordfish and went to the men's room. It had a sign on the door which said "Buoys." Next to it was the ladies' room ("Gulls"). Roger's head ached. He wasn't used to this much booze this fast. Though he'd never been seasick in his life, he thought of tomorrow, sixty miles offshore in a rolling Bertram with the smell of bait, beer and cigars. It made him queasy.

He started back to the bar. There was a crowd at the table now. Ernie had bought more rounds and there were two untouched drinks at Roger's place. He decided he needed some fresh air. He stepped back into the hall and moved over to the open side door. It let in a warm breeze that smelled of beach roses and dune grass. He felt better immediately.

The wall here was also covered with photographs, but of a later vintage. All in color and mostly Polaroid, the pictures were random and haphazard, as if they'd been taken by a child with a new camera. There was Tony behind the bar, Tony's wife holding a mutt, the kitchen stove, the kitchen sink, a Chevy pickup, kittens, girls clowning, a high-school band on parade, a young girl's basketball team, a priest, a boy at the oars of a skiff, a close-up of a sea robin dangling from the end of a line, a fire hydrant painted red, white and blue, a cruising sailboat on a mooring and Tony behind the bar with his back to the camera.

Roger looked at the picture of the sailboat on the mooring. It didn't have the quality of Seaman Lacombe's work but it was certainly familiar: the cutaway forefoot, the straight sheer, the reverse transom, the flush deck forward, the winch island, the self-steering vane. The name hadn't been painted on the side yet but Roger knew the boat was *Hound of Ulster*. He fetched Tony.

"Oh, Christ," Tony said, "them snaps is all Debbie's. I got her that camera for her birthday last year. Lemme see if she's in the kitchen."

Debbie was thirteen and effusive. She wore a small chef's cap over her dark hair and smiled broadly at Roger.

"How ya doin'?" she said. Tony went back to the bar.

"I really like your pictures," said Roger.

"No shit? I got more in the back."

He asked her if she could remember when she took the picture of the sailboat. She thought for a moment.

"Sure. Me and Erline took almost a whole roll at the Xavier tag sale. It was about a week before St. Patrick's Day. That one of the band was on the same roll, and the basketball team and Father Novak. We had a picture left, so we took the sailboat on the way home. Come out good, huh?

"Yes," said Roger.

St. Patrick's Day. March 17. Then the picture had been taken

67

about March 10, right at the beginning of Con's qualification trial for the OSTAR. The OSTAR committee required that each contestant show he was qualified to enter the single-handed ocean race by completing a five-hundred-mile offshore passage alone. Most contestants on the East Coast had sailed to Bermuda the summer before with a sworn affidavit from someone that the passage had been made solo.

But no one sailed to Bermuda in March. In fact, no one in his right mind went offshore in March. But Con had run out of time. To qualify he would have to sail 250 miles straight into the ocean and back and, as proof of passage, submit his plot, log and sextant sights to the OSTAR office.

The first two weeks of March had been the worst in a half century. Winds were gale force from the NE, seas mountainous and the temperature in the upper thirties, which made hypothermia a real threat. Under those circumstances no one would have blamed Con for stopping in Montauk Lake to get some rest before going around the point into the ocean.

"Hell, no," said Debbie. "The boat was here a lot longer'n that. It was on Joe Yedresek's winter mooring for about a week. Maybe more. The man closed her up, paid Joe and took off. It was at least a week. You can ask Joe."

Roger remembered now that after Con had returned from his qualification trial, Griff Monday had brought *Hound*'s main and jib into the office to have the numbers put on. Griff remarked that the sails looked like the boat'd never left the dock. The spreader and pulpit patches were clean and there was no distortion of the cloth at the reef cringles.

Roger asked directions to Joe Yedresek's house.

The house would have been hard to see without the street light in front of it. It was part of a two-family dwelling, cream brick and stucco with the wood trim around the windows painted glossy green. Country music came through the open doorway and Roger could see reflections from a television set flickering on the wall inside. He tried the doorbell. It didn't work. He knocked on the screen. After a moment, a lanky blonde came out. She was about thirty-five, gaunt but bosomy. She wore jeans and a T-shirt that proclaimed "Sex is better than bowling . . . the balls are smaller and you don't have to change your shoes."

"Good evening," Roger said. I'm looking for Joe Yedresek."

She surveyed his rugby shirt, his curly blond hair and mustache, his Breton red shorts and scuffed Topsiders worn without socks.

"Joe ain't here," she said. "I'm his wife. Come on in."

Roger followed her into the front room. The TV was tuned to a Mets game with the sound turned down. Country music came from a record player plugged into a standing lamp.

"I'm really his widow," she said.

"Oh, I'm sorry."

"He ain't dead. He just ain't here. He scallops and quahogs and longlines and drags. Whatever. Name it, he does it. And when he ain't fishin' he drives a semi. My name's Frieda. What's yours?"

"Roger."

"Hiya. Would you like a soda or something stronger? I'm having a lee-cure."

Roger watched her pour him a Pepsi. She was barefoot. Her dyed hair, which came almost to her waist, needed washing. She didn't wear a bra under the T-shirt and her big breasts fidgeted beneath the thin cotton cloth when she moved. Frieda Yedresek was the kind of girl Roger's mother would have called "ordinary." That meant, among other things, that she wasn't descended from English Protestant stock. When Roger was in his teens, his mother steadfastly pointed him at "nice" girls: girls who wore braces, girls who were taller than he, lockjawed girls and girls who rode horses and took piano lessons. Roger, just as steadfastly, resisted them and sought the company of young secretaries, nurses, and dental assistants; professionals and ordinary girls all of them.

Frieda sat on the floor with her legs tucked under her. She vaguely remembered the sailboat on Joe's mooring. She thinks the man paid Joe thirty-nine dollars (a dollar a foot, Roger thought). She agreed the boat must've been there a week or more.

"But I don't know these things. I'm an indoor girl," she said,

69

reaching over her shoulder to scratch an itch. She looked at Roger's beat-up deck moccasins.

"You don't look like no fisherman."

Roger shook his head. "I run a boatyard in Connecticut."

"Connecticut is nice," she said.

"I helped build that sailboat on Joe's mooring."

She scratched the other shoulder. "I guess if you can build a boat, you ain't no fruit, huh?"

Roger was delighted. He laughed.

She smiled. One of her front teeth was chipped. The Loretta Lynn record ended. She crawled over to the record player. Roger finished his Pepsi and got up to leave.

She was selecting a Tammy Wynette record when she was suddenly afflicted with a need to scratch the two inaccessible shoulder blades again. She dropped the record and struggled to her feet.

"Jesus!" she said.

Roger watched helplessly.

"Oh, my God!" she cried. "It's hives. Help me!"

Roger found the two places just inboard of her shoulder blades and scratched. Her relief was immense. After a few moments, her head sagged forward and she exhaled.

"Thanks. Jesus, that was awful. Must be an allergy or something. Maybe the raspberry cordial."

Her voice dropped to a whisper. Roger was still rubbing the two spots on her back when she slowly turned around inside his hands and took off the T-shirt.

A double bed filled the tiny room. The street light outside gave her body a twilight luminescense.

"Learn me," she murmured in the semidarkness. For an hour they did nothing but explore and caress, stroke and kiss. It was something new for Roger. She compelled him to be patient. Once, when he drifted off into some private enjoyment and forgot about her for a moment, she tapped him on the nose and brought him back. She made him pay attention. He began to feel the pleasant, throbbing return of a lost resource.

But, when she finally spread her long thighs and drew him

inside, he took it as a signal to stop paying attention and start performing. He began to plunge. She seized him by the hip bones and stopped him.

"Hey," she said. "Where you goin'? You got another date or somethin'?" She stroked his hair. "Shhh. Drive slow or you'll have an accident."

For almost another hour she kept him on edge. She gave him love lessons. Finally, when she knew his power was at its peak, she slowly raised her knees, grasped the top of the mattress and thought about Joe Yedresek's muscular forearms. She thrust deep, then, and cried out. Roger vortexed. His body detonated and rocked. For what seemed an eternity, he thought he was going to fall. He moaned and held on. She thrust and thrust. And then she wept.

Afterward, wreathed in goosebumps and longing for sleep, he collapsed beside her. When he awoke at daybreak she was gone. There was a note on her pillow.

Work ½ day Sats. Coffee and danish on stove. Thanks for fixing my ich. Your terrific. F.

He got up, took a shower in the plastic curtained tub and drank a cup of coffee from her battered percolator. The kitchen was depressing. It was dark and smelled of oilcloth and sour dish towels. But nothing could discourage Roger this morning. On the contrary, he was almost lightheaded. Frieda had returned his swindled virility. The specter of Katya had been exorcised. Roger felt cured, like an outpatient.

He went to the dockmaster's office at the Deep Sea Club and left a note for Ernie together with a check for his share of the charter. Then he caught the ferry and drove to Newport.

# CHAPTER 12

Des Macroth and Marshall Leonetti walked over the wild tract of woodland and waterfront that was to become the Shinnecossett Recreation Facility. A year ago, when the sealed bids were submitted, it was generally believed the seven-figure construction contract would go to either Smedley & Foote, an old New Haven firm, or Chapin & Sons, a Norwich company with state-house connections. That was before Marshall Leonetti loaned Con the hundred thousand and landed on the board at Macroth.

The two men walked down to the water where the marina would be built. A pair of blackbacked gulls were arguing over a dead eel. One had it by the head, the other by the tail. There was a raucous tug of war.

Standing on the dark sand, Des could almost see the entire

property. It had been private for a hundred years, held in trust for another twenty and, finally, given to the state for tax reasons. For as long as Des could remember, the land had been the center of a controversy between developers and environmentalists and, after the zoning board eventually gave its approval, between the developers themselves ... notably Len Smedley and George Chapin. That Macroth had walked off with the contract was miraculous. It mystified and frightened Des.

"I'm overwhelmed," he said quietly to Leonetti. "How on earth did you manage it?"

There was a cry as one of the gulls let go its end of the eel. The other lost its balance, fell backward, flapping, and was immediately set upon by its opponent. While the two birds were thus engaged, a third gull made off with the eel.

"That's how," said Leonetti cheerfully.

But, of course, it wasn't as simple as that.

Marshall Leonetti was a man of many hats. That he was able to wear them all successfully, sometimes even simultaneously, was a tribute to his skill as an entrepreneur. He belonged, for example, to the TWU and the American Rifle Association but was also local representative of the Sierra Club. He owned a fleet of rental vehicles—pickup trucks, forklifts, road graders and mobile mixers—but he also cochaired the southeastern Connecticut Wetlands Commission. He relied on his family. His wife, Donna, came from third-generation gravel and traprock, a family which, by marriage, was related to plate glass. In the family, too, was a cousin in asphalt and an uncle in concrete. Marshall also relied on friendship. His college roommate was a state assemblyman and an attorney for the EPA.

Leonetti was motivated by profit the way some people are motivated by sex or danger. That's why he owned the Meriden Jai Alai. It's also why he made the deal with Con Macroth. There was no vicarious excitement for Leonetti in backing an ocean racer. He did it purely for profit.

"My marine guy took a look at those photographs of the *Hound* you sent over," he said to Des as they returned to the silver Bentley. "He estimates the boat is still worth a hundred fifty or a hundred seventy-five undamaged." He unlocked the car doors, got in and looked at himself in the rear-view mirror.

"It's a shame about Con's accident," he said, touching his curly red hair. "I mean that sincerely. But I'm not going to be stuck with the boat. I want it back and on the market. My nephew, Archer, is on his way to Newfoundland. The kid can see in the fog."

Roger spent the day in Newport. Through an English friend, temporarily employed by OSTAR, he managed to get a look at the material Con had submitted in March as proof of his single-handed 500-miler.

There were two charts, 13205 and 13218 as well as DMA Plotting Sheet 905 (38 degrees to 44 degrees). A dozen photocopied Power Squadron 229 sight-reduction forms and several logbook pages were rolled up in the charts and secured with masking tape. To Roger, the material looked as if it had never been opened.

Con had done his homework on the plotting sheet. With great care, he had drawn in Montauk Light, Fire Island, Cape Henlopen, Delaware, Block Island SE Light, Point Jude, Brenton Tower, Beavertail and Castle Hill. He'd plotted a course that took him downwind from Montauk to a point southeast of Cape Henlopen (about two hundred miles from Montauk). There he'd altered to the east for perhaps fifty miles and then to the northeast which took him straight back to Newport. Total distance was about five hundred miles.

The voyage, according to the log pages, had taken four days. Noon sights were entered on the plotting sheet each day. Roger checked the sight-reduction forms. They were immaculate. Equally tidy were several morning sun lines for longitude which had been advanced to noon for running fixes. In the log, Con gave hourly speeds to 0.1 knot and compass courses to one degree of accuracy.

It was all malarkey.

The wind had been gale force from the northeast throughout the period. No sailboat can sail northeast in a northeaster without tacking. And few sailboats would have been able to tack to windward in that sea let alone cover a hundred miles a day, which Con's plot showed.

The sights were faked. In a boat with a height of eye of eleven feet, it would have been virtually impossible to get a clear horizon. More to the point, sun sights cannot be had unless the navigator can see the sun. The surface weather maps for the period showed the sun to be totally or partially obscured.

Con had gone into the Nautical Almanac and pulled out the GHA of the sun which corresponded to meridian passage at his invented longitudes, introduced a reasonable intercept error and plotted them. For his morning lines he'd worked backward from Table 25 in Bowditch. It was all bullshit. Like a schoolboy writing a book report from the dust jacket.

Roger felt an elation that was new to him. Ordinarily, when he encountered cheating, it embarrassed or saddened him. This was different. The excitement he felt came from an instinctive certainty that he'd unraveled the first thread in a whole pattern of deceit.

He returned the material, thanked his friend and phoned Barbara.

"How was Spencer's meeting with Connecticut Provident?" he asked.

"Spencer said they gave him two martinis, a london broil and a mild slap on the wrist," Barbara answered. "Anyway, they're going to stand behind him. It may cost him a little. Why aren't you fishing?"

There was a silence. Roger blushed. He hadn't blushed since he farted in church when he was ten.

"Hello?" she said.

"I got waylaid," he said and instantly regretted it.

"Anybody I know?"

He rallied. "Don't be a smartass. Listen. The reason I called. Could we have supper tonight with Spencer? Your place or the schooner. Doesn't matter. And don't fuss. I have extraordinary news which can't wait."

"Give me a hint," she said.

"Not until I see you."

"Truly," complained Barbara, "you will drive me into old age before my time."

He pictured her, resting her cheek in her hand, her full mouth in a half smile, her eyes warm as Christmas windows. "I miss you," he said hoarsely.

Barbara skipped a breath. "That *is* extraordinary news," she murmured. "Hurry home please."

It took her a half hour to make the lobster salad and prepare the garlic bread. But it took nearly the whole afternoon to remake the yellow sundress from St. Pierre. It was two sizes too large (the St. Pierre saleslady had looked at Roger and decided he went with a fourteen).

She fixed the dress, scrubbed the apartment and scrubbed herself. Betsy was mildly diverted. She glanced over her shoulder as her mother stepped, dripping, from the shower. "Gads, I didn't know you could whistle," she said.

When Roger and Spencer arrived, Barbara was finishing her face in the bathroom mirror. She noticed a rosy disk beginning to spread beneath each tanned cheekbone.

"Frig! I'm glowing like a beacon," she muttered.

Roger thought she never looked more beautiful. He was bursting with news and dying to tell it. But he couldn't take his eyes off her. He was sweet and solicitous. He helped serve. He pulled out her chair and helped clear. Spencer watched all this with interest.

When Betsy finally went off to the early movie with Derdriu, Barbara turned to Roger. "Okay, spill it before you explode."

Roger told them about Oscar's, that he'd seen the photo of *Hound* in Montauk and that, according to witnesses, she'd been there a week or more in early March when she was supposed to be at sea on her qualification trial. He described the falsified charts and other documents in Newport.

Spencer received the news soberly and in silence. He tapped out his pipe, refilled it, lit it and relit it several times.

"You're absolutely sure of your facts?" he asked.

"Absolutely."

"Don't you think the qualification committee knows all the tricks of falsifying?"

"Sure," Roger said. "But I don't think they looked at his stuff. Father, it was all taped together and the tape hadn't been disturbed. When I pulled it off it tore the pulp from the back of one of the charts."

Spencer puffed in silence. "Couldn't the snapshot have been of some other Rushton thirty-nine?"

"In March? In Montauk Lake? With an Aries vane?"

Barbara interrupted. "Really, Spence. That's like saying 'Couldn't the snapshot have been of some other purple and orange 1930 Pierce Arrow?'"

Spencer smiled. "Okay, you bastards. I'm only trying to play the devil's goddam advocate. And I'll tell you why. I'm against muckraking. It always hurts and it almost never helps. What good is this information? If Con had won the race, maybe a competitor would've been justified in protesting him on the basis of it. Otherwise what the hell good is it? It won't bring back the boat. It won't bring Con back. He's just as dead now as he was before you went to Oscar's."

"I think what Roger is saying," said Barbara quietly, "is that if Con could fake the qualifying trial, he could fake the rest."

The phone rang. Barbara pushed the office extension button and answered.

"Truly's. Yes, Lieutenant Quinn."

She listened and took notes for almost a minute. Finally she said "Okay" and "Thank you, Lieutenant" and hung up. She took a deep breath.

"That was Bill Quinn from Coast Guard Rescue Coordinating in New York. The Norwegian freighter *Oslofjord* sighted *Hound* this afternoon and took her aboard. They're bringing her in. They'll be at Pier Nine, Brooklyn, Friday morning. *Hound*'s mast has been broken in three places and she's been vandalized. Lieutenant Quinn suggests we be there with counsel and a surveyor to determine her value and to deal with the Norwegians who are claiming salvage."

77

# PART THREE

# HOUND OF ULSTER

# CHAPTER 13

It was eight A.M. and the temperature was already over ninety degrees. Roger, Barbara and Des stood on the sidewalk beside the cars parked in front of Cath's house. They were waiting to drive to Brooklyn. Cath had not yet appeared.

In Roger's VW bus were Spencer and Con's father, Damon. The old man refused to ride in the same car with Cath. "She makes me carsick!" he muttered. "And the bitch is always late!"

In the back seat of the silver, air-conditioned Bentley, Marshall Leonetti, whom Roger and Barbara had just met, sat with his lawyer, Bernard Roth. Des had to yell through the closed windows to introduce them. Leonetti acknowledged Roger with a nod, Barbara with a smile and turned back to his lawyer. Behind the wheel of the Bentley, Leonetti's nephew, Arch, still

81

suffering from jet lag, dozed intermittently. The recovery of *Hound* by the Norwegians had curtailed his trip to Newfoundland.

Des went into the house to see what was delaying Cath. Roger had already begun to sweat. He glanced at the freshly seersuckered Leonetti reclining in air-conditioned comfort.

"Do you think he's in the Mafia?" he murmured to Barbara.

"Why? Because he's a rich Italian?"

"Sure."

"Sweet redneck, dear, there are tons of rich Italians who are not in the Mafia."

"Without hesitating, name three," he said.

"Yogi Berra, Anna Maria Alberghetti and Chef Boyardee."

Roger laughed and took her hand. Cath and Des came out then. Neither Roger nor Barbara was prepared for Cath's costume. She was in mourning. Old-fashioned mourning: black shoes and stockings, black midcalf chiffon dress, black hat with veil pulled back to show the luminous pale skin and dark eyes. She came over to Barbara who had volunteered to stay behind to mind the two girls. Cath whispered a few last minute instructions and disappeared with Des into the Bentley.

"Be safe," said Barbara. Roger kissed her on the cheek, hopped into the VW bus and drove off. The Bentley followed.

Damon Macroth talked all the way to New York. He had a new audience and was going to make the most of it.

"The bitch is always late!" he said again. "I perceive her pattern of tardiness to be . . . genetic . . . or perhaps prenatal . . . or both." He leaned forward and placed his elbows on the back of the front seat.

"It is alleged," he said, "that her father was late for his coital appointment with her mother. The latter had been waiting in the conjugal bed for days, sipping madeira and swatting flies."

Spencer nudged Roger and lit his pipe. The old man continued. "When, at last, his lordship appeared, bearing his bimonthly erection in a velvet cloth like the Kohinoor diamond, he mounted her ladyship and, by some miracle of leverage which

God only knows, managed a climax." Damon tapped Spencer on the shoulder and lowered his voice conspiratorially. "I ask you, sir, to imagine the race of aristocratic sperms up the Grand Canal. First, however, it is necessary to understand the upper-class Englishman.

"The normal, non-British male, upon ejaculation, produces thousands of wiggling little creatures which all crowd into the tunnel at once and head north for Phallopia. This is not so with the upper-class Englishman. The upper-class Englishman produces half a dozen wigglies. No more. He's that cheap! Well." Damon sat back and resumed his declamatory style.

"The patrician egg is waiting. The small band of English public-school sperms start running. The cry of 'Foul!' is heard at every turn of the course. After a few furlongs, a leader is established. He steps on the gas and goes in front by a few lengths. It looks as if he has a clear field. But wait! A challenger has appeared. In the stretch now, the challenger is coming up fast. There's a finish-line sprint by the upstart, a wee bantam sperm with a sweet disposition and quite good legs. Alas! At the last second he is impaled upon a minor uterine cyst. The leader, the real upper-class fish, unchallenged now, strong and snotty, plunges into the egg sac like a Poseidon missile, exploding and scattering militancy, emotional bankruptcy and congenital tardiness to the four walls of the amnionic sac. The race is over. Ten months and one week later, Cath is born. Sure, she was late for her birth and has been late ever since!"

Spencer applauded.

Behind them, the Bentley cruised along in silence, as advertised. Cath could hear the clock tick. At the Greenwich toll booth, Leonetti opened a tiny refrigerator and produced freshly made caponata which he served on Italian bread with a bottle of Orvieto.

By the time the convoy crossed the Throg's Neck Bridge, the day had clouded over and become cooler. On the BQE it started to rain and, at Pier 9, Brooklyn, it was pouring.

They huddled under the pier's corrugated roof and tried to

avoid the leaks. *Oslofjord* had been delayed in Gravesend Bay but was now picking up her tug off Governor's Island and would be alongside within twenty minutes. Roger looked around him at the serious faces.

Marshall Leonetti's face was blank. Roger had heard he wanted a hundred fifty or a hundred seventy-five thousand for *Hound.* The salvage figure awarded the Norwegians would be important to him. Of Leonetti's lawyer, Roth, Roger knew nothing. He was a rough-looking man with bushy eyebrows and none of Leonetti's suavity. Arch Leonetti looked sleepy and laid back. As far as Roger could tell he was simply an employee who chauffeured his uncle and would probably rather be sailing. Des and Cath stood arm in arm, pale and silent, poised to view the remains. Only Professor Macroth, on the brink of a kind of hilarious and furious senility, seemed to be enjoying himself in spite of the occasion. Then there was Spencer, Roger's father, liable for part of the salvage claim, beloved and vulnerable.

Off to one side, beyond the waiting longshoremen, was another group, more solemn-faced than the rest.

"Lawyers and insurance people," said Spencer nervously. He muttered out of the side of his mouth. "Specialists in the profitable handling of other people's misfortune. Wish we didn't need 'em but we do."

They were people Roger didn't know. One, a tall, studious-looking man in oval, steel-rimmed glasses, detached himself from the group and came over. He was about Roger's age and wore a light, zippered raincoat, rubbers over his cordovans and a gray fedora.

"Spencer Truly?" he asked.

Spencer nodded.

He removed his hat and introduced himself. He was Norton Garrison of the Admiralty Law Firm of Bishop, English and James who had been retained by the Connecticut Provident Insurance Company for the purpose of negotiating a salvage figure.

"Salvor is not represented by counsel," he said. His voice was measured and precise except for a slight eastern-school attenuation at the vowels. "We'll be dealing directly with Captain Jacobsen. Our marine surveyor met the ship with the pilot and will have a preliminary yacht survey prepared by the time they're alongside. I . . . ah . . . foresee no difficulties." With that he nodded, carefully replaced his hat and rejoined his group.

The longshoremen began walking down the pier. Roger looked out on the river and saw *Oslofjord* moving slowly across the current, nuzzled by her tug. In a few minutes she entered the slip. *Hound* lay on the freighter's foredeck, like a beached, dead whale. Her topsides were scarred and gouged, her boot top foul with weed and her bottom covered with gooseneck barnacles to the turn of the bilge. Her port stanchions were bent inboard and her stern pulpit had been torn off. The freighter looked more like a yacht than the yacht. She was freshly painted light gray with her superstructure buff. The foreside of her bridge was varnished tongue and groove cedar and her lifeboats were clinker built and finished bright. Whistles sounded. The ship, next to the pier now, lost way and stopped. Bow, stern, spring and breast heaving lines snaked ashore at almost precisely the moment she let go her outboard anchor. The seamanship was impressive, contrasting sharply with the last time Roger saw an American-owned Liberian come alongside and nearly wipe out Hoboken.

He wished Barbara were with him. She was missing something. To Barbara, missing something was worse than being embezzled. When Roger sailed with her, offshore at night, she'd stand her watch and the next and the next, denying herself sleep for fear of missing something. Anything. A shooting star. She seemed hooked into life's circulatory system; like a vital organ. "Wish you were here," he said, echoing a cliché as old as love.

They went aboard, Cath and Des first. Cath paused at the top of the gangplank and gazed at the wounded yacht lashed down to padeyes in the well deck by the main hatch. Standing there in the rain, she looked regal and full of catastrophe, a desolate queen at the funeral of her liege. Roger felt compassion for her in spite of his suspicions.

Their group was directed to the ship's saloon. Next to a long table, the steward had set up a coffee urn. The smell of the fresh brew filled the deck space. Helping himself to a cup was an elderly man with a small round body beneath a large, round, bald head. He was wearing a policeman's rain cape many sizes too large for him.

"Cliff Leonard, you nice old son of a bitch!" cried Spencer.

Cliff Leonard turned and twinkled at Spencer through ancient, highly polished pince-nez glasses. When he was pleased he shook his head and the glasses wiggled on his nose, casting shards of light which danced about on the saloon walls like Tinker Bell. Cliff, about Spencer's age, had been a lawyer, a coast-artillery officer, a writer of marine insurance and a life-insurance investigator. Above all, he was a freighter buff. He probably knew more about freighters than any man in the world. He voyaged in them, wrote about them, photographed them and, when he could, met them in the lower bay aboard the pilot boat. Running into Spencer on *Oslofjord* seemed the happiest coincidence. Roger left the two men with their coffee and went on deck. He walked forward to where *Hound* lay.

Norton Garrison stood next to the yacht talking to a young man in chinos and deck shoes. Roger knew the man slightly. He was Bill Carlson, a prominent yacht surveyor and measurer from the western end of the sound.

"She was picked pretty clean," Carlson said. "What was left the Norwegians removed and inventoried. Apparently there are four or five bags of stuff locked in the captain's cabin."

Roger climbed the sloping deck of the yacht and stood in the cockpit. All but two winches were gone. There wasn't a cleat left. The compasses and all the instruments . . . windspeed, apparent wind, Kenyon . . . were gone. The boom, spinnaker pole and mast, in three jagged pieces, were lashed to the starboard stanchions. The anemometer and masthead vane had been stripped off. Only the wire remained. On deck, all that was left were the two dorade boxes with their neoprene ventilators. Below there was nothing. Even the little two-burner stove had been taken.

"What about charts?" Roger asked.

"In the captain's cabin," Carlson said.

Apart from the obvious destruction and loss of equipment and hardware, Carlson's survey showed the damage to be nonintegral and cosmetic. The hull and deck, at least, were sound. Roger guessed that, sometime between *Bearn* and *Oslofjord,* a steel ship or large fishing vessel had made fast alongside *Hound* in a seaway. With the pounding the yacht must have taken, it was a miracle she wasn't sent to the bottom. For a split second, Roger pictured Marshall Leonetti flying his nephew to Newfoundland, not to bring *Hound* home but to sink her. Of course it was absurd. There hadn't been time.

Spencer called out from the main deck. He placed four fingers on his sleeve and pointed inside the ship. The captain had appeared.

Several white canvas bags and rolls of charts had been placed on the long saloon table behind which stood Captain Jacobsen and two of his officers. The Norwegian captain was an old man by American Merchant Marine standards; probably over seventy. But he was tall ... the tallest man in the room ... strong and straight with hands the size of dinner plates and light blue eyes set in a face as stern as a Lutheran Sunday. He was, however, meticulously courteous. When it was apparent everyone was present, he asked them to be seated. In excellent English he introduced himself, his mate and his chief engineer. These men had supervised the removal of personal belongings from the yacht and placed them in canvas bags, each labeled with its contents. He now requested the owners to examine each of the bags and check its contents against the mate's manifest to see that nothing was missing. Bernard Roth spoke briefly to Cath and Des. They agreed to waive examination. The manifest was then placed before Cath for signing. She stared at the sheet of paper which had been neatly typed under the ship's letterhead.

1 spool thread, black
1 packet steel needles, sewing

8 tins stew, beef
1 glove, left hand, wool
etc.

The captain handed her his pen. She looked at him inquisitively for a moment then abruptly signed the paper, accepting, for all practical purposes, what was left of Con Macroth.

The bags and charts were removed to a corner of the saloon. The captain sat down and placed his merchant-navy hat with the faded gold crown on the table.

"Who to represent the insurers?" he asked.

"Bishop, English," said Norton Garrison, handing the captain his card.

Captain Jacobsen examined the card. "Very well, Mr. Garrison. Shall we proceed?"

Garrison nodded.

"My owners, Norsk-Flag," said Jacobsen, "have instructed me to accept no less than $250,000 to release the yacht *Hound of Ulster*."

"Jesus!" said Spencer, under his breath.

Roger saw Leonetti lean back and look at the ceiling. Garrison, who was leafing through some papers, never blinked.

Bernard Roth stood up. "As counsel for the owners," Roth began.

"Will counsel identify himself?" intoned Garrison, wearily. He made Roth give his full name, firm name, firm address, phone number and zip code. Roger thought he saw the trace of a smile appear on the captain's weathered face.

"As counsel for the owners," Roth continued, "I believe the figure requested by Captain Jacobsen is entirely proper, approximating, as it does, the insured value of the yacht plus *Oslofjord*'s labor, fuel expended, time lost, et cetera. The figure is realistic and fair. It is acceptable to us."

Garrison did not rise. Instead he fixed Roth with that special look of disdain which, it is alleged, is a prerequisite for graduation from the Harvard Law School.

"Mr. Roth," he said, as if Roth had just committed a nuisance

on the carpet, "your reasoning is chimerical, sir. Indeed, the figure the captain has named and you support substantially exceeds
the insured value of the yacht for total loss, a figure which in no
way reflects her sound value as she lies." He let his gaze wander
around the table. "*Absit invidia,* gentlemen. The salvor's right
to award is indisputable. But, if you please, let us examine the
criteria."

He opened a folder, found the page he wanted and read aloud.
"The criteria for salvage award include: 'Labor and skill dem-
onstrated by the salvor, degree of damage to salvor's property,
risk and extent of danger from which insured property was saved
and, finally, value of the saved property' . . . *Admiralty Law,* Bis-
pham and Gridley, Second Edition."

Roth sat down. Garrison closed the folder. "There was neither
danger nor risk to the salvor's property or personnel," he said.
"Inasmuch as the sea was calm and recovery took less than two
hours, the only criterion with which we need concern ourselves
is the one of value of the saved property. Mr. William Carlson,
marine surveyor of this city, has placed a value of thirty thousand
dollars on the yacht as she lies."

Roth snorted.

"I for one," said Garrison languidly, "feel the figure is high.
The yacht was fashioned for single-handed sailing. It will take
many additional thousands to convert her to regular cruising-
racing trim. However. My client has authorized me to submit the
figure of thirty thousand dollars *ad interim,* that is for a letter of
undertaking releasing the yacht to the owners pending later survey and negotiation by both insurers and salvors."

"I object a lot," said Roth. "I don't have to be an admiralty
lawyer to see the boat has a couple scratches. But thirty thousand
is a laugh. I object."

Garrison removed his glasses and massaged his eyes. "Mr.
Roth, this is not a court of law. Your objection is a matter of
complete indifference to me as it is perfectly plain your inten-
tions are to hyperbolize the yacht's value for purposes of resale."
He replaced his glasses and turned to Captain Jacobsen.

"Captain, the longer *Hound of Ulster* lies against your number-one hatch the longer it will take to offload your cargo. While she is aboard your vessel, she is your responsibility. I worry about your turn-around schedule, sir." For the first time, Norton Garrison smiled. *"Nunc aut nunquam,"* he said. "The longshoremen go on overtime at five."

Cath watched the straps tighten and hug the yacht's hull as the ship's big cargo boom took the strain and she was lifted and swung across the deck as easily as a bale of straw. She hung high over the side, blotting out the sun for an instant. The electric winch rattled then, and she dropped quickly, disappearing beyond the ship's bulwarks into the oily river below. A Coast Guard patrol boat took her in tow for City Island. She'd lie there until Griff and Bryan, already on their way west in the yard workboat, would tow her home to Sandwich.

Leonetti and Roth left the ship without speaking to anyone. The captain waited at the gangplank for Cath. Towering over her, he removed his hat, bowed slightly and kissed her hand. It was a scene ancient as the sea.

Roger offered to take the canvas bags and charts. He, Spencer and Cliff Leonard lugged them ashore and carefully placed them in the back of the VW bus. Damon Macroth, wanting to be useful, brought the charts off the ship. However, he'd heard about the air conditioning and the wine and, Cath notwithstanding, elected to return to Sandwich aboard the Bentley.

It had stopped raining. The streets were steaming. Roger and Spencer gave Cliff Leonard a lift to the Clark Street subway station. Cliff, it turned out, was not aboard *Oslofjord* solely to satisfy his lifelong lust for freighters. He was also there on business.

Egality Corporation, a large life-insurance investigation firm, had been requested by one of the carriers of Con's life insurance to look into the matter of Con's disappearance. Egality asked Cliff to do the investigation.

"I think they're all guilty as hell," Spencer now said. "Guilty as hell. I hope you nail 'em."

Cliff shook his head cheerfully. The light danced off his pince-nez.

"My friend," he said, "big insurance companies like to think of themselves as monolithic and impregnable. They become agitated at anything that might dispel that image. In general, although they dislike losing money, they prefer ... like the Victorians ... to close ranks and absorb the loss rather than admit publicly they've been defrauded."

Roger pulled over to the subway entrance and double-parked. Cliff continued. "We have here four big insurance carriers with combined assets of about thirty *billion*. To them, the loss of a million and a half is a drop in the bucket."

"A million and a half?" asked Roger.

"Oh sure," said Cliff, sparkling. "Con Macroth was insured for a million, five hundred thousand dollars."

# CHAPTER 14

A few minutes after Barbara received Roger's midmorning call from Brooklyn, Griff and Bryan fired up the old workboat, *Yardbird*, and headed for City Island. Barbara left the watchman and boss painter in charge of Truly's and walked back to Cath's house.

Derdriu and Betsy had made spaghetti sauce so Cath wouldn't have to cook when she got home. The kitchen stove, the counters and the walls were spattered with red shrapnel, as if a tomato pie had exploded. They'd made enough spaghetti sauce to feed half the lower valley. Eventually, most of it was given away. They gave some to Spencer who was going to a BYOB potluck supper at the yacht club. They gave a quart to Barbara. They even offered some to Mr. Narducci, the letter carrier, when he delivered the insured parcel. He politely declined the sauce but, while Derdriu was signing for the parcel, asked if he might have the postmark. Mr. Narducci collected postmarks from all over the world but he'd never seen one from St. Pierre and Miquelon.

Barbara's little apartment over the boatyard office had once been an attic. Like all attics it was under the roof and hot. Barbara didn't like air-conditioning, so a large, screened skylight was installed in the gambrel. It provided light and ventilation and, thanks to a boatyard ladder, access to the roof for sitting, dreaming and river watching. Barbara called it her treehouse.

It was early evening and the caravan had returned from New York. The air was still and smelled of honeysuckle, river bottom and spaghetti sauce. Barbara and Roger sat on the roof, sipped their drinks and watched a flight of swans move slowly up the river, mythical birds upon a green embroidery. The moment was idyllic. But Barbara had come down with a terrible case of the shies.

She'd watched the clock all day for Roger's return. All day she'd marshaled her expectations and desires with a kind of elated brazenness. She knew Betsy was spending the night with Derdriu and that, for the first time since his ... renaissance, Roger and she would be alone. She savored the anticipation. She fantasized. But when Roger finally parked the bus and stood before her, her boldness deserted her and she was almost incapacitated by shyness.

Perched next to her on the roof, Roger excitedly told her about the *Oslofjord* meeting from the beginning: how he'd missed her, how the freighter looked, how *Hound* looked and how Garrison had dominated the negotiations. Barbara, wearing short shorts and a fitted blue-jean shirt, felt naked. She couldn't decide what to do with her legs. Roger told her about Cliff Leonard and Con's million-dollar insurance policy. Barbara only half listened. Either the blue-jean shirt had shrunk or her breasts had grown. She lowered her gaze when he looked at her. She giggled. At one point, when there was a lull in the conversation, she found herself humming.

"Jesus," she said finally, a drink sooner than usual, "let's eat!" They climbed down the ladder.

Roger concentrated on her face as she poured the wine. He was trying to program himself to remember her face exactly. He hadn't remembered it in Brooklyn. Not exactly. For when he got home, it was a notch lovelier.

Dinner seemed to go on for about a minute. Suddenly the dishes were done and Roger was taking the garbage down the outside stairs to the dumpster. When he returned she was standing in the middle of the kitchen with nothing left to do. Her hands were clasped behind her and she was simply standing there under the ceiling light, her eyes in shadow. Roger felt the soles of his feet prickle. He gazed at her and wondered if she could hear his heart beating.

"Barbara."

She took a long, slow breath. "Yes."

"I love you."

She lowered her head. He went to her and took her face in his hands. There was a single tear on one of her lashes. He kissed it away. He kissed her cheeks and hair and eyes and kissed her smile. She locked her arms around his neck and pressed herself against him. They held each other.

"Oh, Roger," she whispered. "Oh, Roger. Oh yes. Oh shit!"


It was as easy and natural as breathing. And it marked the moment that Roger Truly, who was thirty-six, learned the difference between love and lust. It changed him forever.

Barbara fell asleep smiling, a slim brown arm flung across her man's chest. Roger studied her sleeping face and wondered again if he could remember it exactly. But his eyes wouldn't stay open. He lay quietly for a moment and listened to the river rustling. Then he gathered his happiness about him like a quilt and slept.


Barbara, as with most mothers of young children, was a light sleeper. It was she who first heard the pounding on the door. She glanced at her watch. It was almost two A.M. She jumped up and

94

put on the first thing she could find. Roger's rugby shirt. It came to her knees, like a dress. The pounding was persistent.

"All right, already," she muttered. She ran to the door, switched on the outside light and peered through the curtain. Her heart stopped. It was Betsy, in her pajamas. Barbara wrenched open the door.

"Betsy!"

"Mom! Come Quick! We think Derd's mom has killed herself!"

Roger and Barbara hurried up Water Street, Roger carrying Betsy piggyback. They first heard Con's voice when they skirted the Congregational Church property and turned into Pleasant Street. Con's voice, amplified a dozen times, boomed down the dark, tree-lined streets of Sandwich, shattering the stillness of the sleeping village. Con's amplified voice boomed down the streets, hoarse and full of trembling declamation.

> "He will be your Hound . . .
> Guard all Murtheimne Plain
> And Cúchulainn shall be his name!"

Roger and Barbara broke into a trot as lights in several houses came on and outraged faces began to appear in windows.

"Listen to the grand feats of the Hound of Ulster!" shouted the voice. "Listen . . . "

At the door of Cath's house, in his bathrobe, stood Cath's next-door neighbor, the Episcopal rector, the Reverend Mr. Townsend. "The screen door is locked," he said helpfully.

Roger put Betsy down, cut through the screen with his rigging knife and went in. The first thing he saw, in the vestibule, was the torn wrapping paper with the sender's address uppermost: "Bureau de Transport Maritime, Dept. de St. Pierre & Miquelon, France, Amerique du Nord." Con's tapes and log had finally arrived.

Next to the tape deck on the living-room floor sat Damon Macroth, grinning from ear to ear and matching, in Gaelic, every word Con was declaiming in English. Roger snapped off the tape machine. "Where's Cath?" he asked Betsy.

"In the kitchen. Derd's upstairs."

Cath lay on the kitchen floor on her back. A half-empty container of Librium stood on the counter by the sink. While Roger upended her over the downstairs toilet, Barbara called Dr. Comstock. Cath coughed up six tablets and some thickish fluid. The doctor, to his credit, arrived almost immediately. He took Cath's pulse, blood pressure, checked her eyes and prescribed black coffee and walking.

"She's okay physically," he said. "She didn't take enough to do the job. I'll call Valley Ambulance and have her admitted for observation at the Shoreline Psychiatric Facility."

The phone rang before the doctor could get to it. Roger answered. It was the Sandwich Police Chief. There'd been a complaint: disturbing the peace.

"All quiet now, Chief," Roger said. "No. No. Just a little domestic problem. Yes. She's okay. Right. See you at Rotary, Chief." Roger hung up. Dr. Comstock made his calls and left.

The Reverend Mr. Townsend and Barbara took turns walking Cath and administering the coffee. For Father Townsend this was an act of the purest Christian charity as Cath had never darkened his congregation nor any other for that matter. Cath was ladylike, behaved passively and did exactly as she was told—until a few minutes before the ambulance arrived. They were in the living room. Damon Macroth had helped himself to a large Paddy's and water without ice. Reverend Townsend was walking Cath. Suddenly she screamed.

"Fedelm!" she screamed. "Fedelm! Fedelm! The son of a bitch is up there screwing that Druid whore Fedelm, leaving me to rot in this cocksucking Wasp shithole! Aaaaaaah! Aaaaaaaah!"

Father Townsend dropped Cath's arm and stood, congealed, in the center of the room.

"Druid whore! Harlot!" she shrieked and waved her fists.

Damon Macroth poured the rector a drink. "Here, Father," he said. "Have a wee jar to steady the nerves and bulwark yer tender sensibilities against yon brutish Anglo-Saxon epithets." The professor turned to Roger. "Pay no attention to her, for God's sake. She's raving. 'Fedelm,' the name she howls, was the poetess of Connacht in Celtic Ireland two thousand years ago. Con mentioned Fedelm on the tape a while back and she went wild."

Cath turned on the old man. "Piss on you!" she hissed. "She's a whore! She's ..." Cath stopped in midsentence and suddenly smiled at her father-in-law. "Ask O'Dandy, you stupid Mick!"

The ambulance arrived. Barbara packed Cath an overnight bag. The lady ambulance driver was a volunteer who worked as a checkout clerk in the local Finast. Cath knew her. She got into the ambulance without a fuss and the orange-and-white vehicle drove off into the night, blinking and flashing haphazardly.

Barbara and Roger went upstairs to Derdriu's room. The dark, curly-haired child sat on the edge of her bed with Betsy. Roger suggested that Derd and Betsy come back to the yard and live on the schooner for a while. "Until your mother's had a couple of days' rest."

"She's crazy," said Derdriu.

Barbara went to her. "She's not, Derd. She's upset. Something on the tape upset her."

Derdriu shook her head. "Everything upsets her. She's crazy!"

"Honey ..."

"She's fucking daft!"

*"Derdriu!"*

The child rolled over on her stomach and burst into tears.

"I want my da!" she cried and buried her face in the pillow.

# CHAPTER 15

She cried for a long time, ending with the hiccups. Barbara rubbed her back and stroked the dark, curly hair. Finally the hiccups subsided. For a moment they thought she was asleep. She wasn't. She rolled over, sat up dry-eyed, and stated that she would not stay on the schooner with Betsy.

"Someone has to look after Grandfather," she said quietly.

Betsy stared at her friend, and without realizing it, grasped her mother's hand.

When they came downstairs, Professor Macroth was asleep on his back on the couch. A half-empty glass of whiskey rested, like the Leaning Tower, on his chest. Barbara removed the glass. Derdriu shook the old man.

"Grandfather. Wake up and go to sleep in your bed."

The furious eye opened and glared at Derdriu.

"Off you go, Papa," she said and patted his thin shoulder. "There's a good lad."

The huge eye closed for a moment. When it opened again it seemed to have lost some of its ferocity. The old man studied Derdriu.

"Very well," he muttered finally. "Very well." They watched as he struggled up from the couch. He got to his feet and walked to the stairs. When he arrived there he stopped.

"Wait," he said. "I must call Desmond."

"Not now, Granda," said Derdriu. "'Tis the middle of the night."

"'Ask O'Dandy, yew stupid Mick!' is what she said to me. 'Ask O'Dandy!'"

"And so you will," said Derdriu calmly. "Tomorrow. But go to your bed now, dear."

The old man gazed down at his granddaughter. He looked over at Barbara, Roger and Betsy and back to his granddaughter. Then, with the faintest trace of twinkle, he turned and climbed the stairs.

Betsy had witnessed this sudden metamorphosis of her best friend with anguish. It was as if Derdriu had taken grown-up pills. Betsy felt forsaken.

But as soon as Damon was upstairs, Derdriu turned to Barbara. "Mrs. Foster," she said, "could Betsy stay and help me with Grandfather?"

Barbara never had a chance to answer. The girls, children again, fell into each other's arms.

It was almost four A.M. when Roger and Barbara returned to the yard with the cassettes and Con's logbook and charts. Now, with the eastern sky just beginning to light the office windows and with the material before him, Roger sensed that same exhilaration he'd felt in Newport when he discovered Con had faked his March qualification trial. Before Newport, he hadn't had much to go on: the missing sextant which, in St. Pierre, Des was so quick to accept as evidence of Con's demise, the missing RDF and the photograph of *Hound* heading east instead of west were all simply isolated inconsistencies that had aroused Roger's seaman's curiosity. It was the faked trial and the fact that Con had disappeared for a week, while *Hound* sat on a mooring in Montauk Lake, that molded Roger's conviction that a deceit had been performed; that Con Macroth had not been lost at sea at all. There were, of course, countless unanswered questions. Neither Marshall Leonetti nor anyone in the Macroth family was likely to spring forward to acknowledge them.

Roger placed the first cassette in the office tape recorder. Perhaps, after all, it was not so much exhilaration he felt than the certain knowledge this was the end of the line. Either the tapes, the log and the charts would supply the answers—or there weren't any answers.

# CHAPTER 16

The cassette was marked "Tape #1, June 5–8."
Roger pressed the start lever.

"*Five June, 1976.*"

(Con's voice is rather formal.)

"*Observer Single-Handed Transatlantic Race ... Rushton sloop Hound of Ulster ... Conchobor Macroth, Master.*"

(There is a rasping noise which sometimes makes Con's remarks indistinct. As this noise only occurs when the tape recorder is in the cockpit, it is diagnosed as wind over the tiny, built-in microphone.)

"*Dear God, what a zoo! The big boats started first, thank heaven! One of them is the size of the QE2!*" (Tooting horns in background.)

"*Our class got off clear enough although someone had to shout for buoy room at the weather end of the line. Spectator boats dropping back. Fair for the Lizard now. Should fetch during the night. Speed 7.2 knots under full main and just started number one.*"

(Break.)

Roger sat at his desk with Con's logbook in front of him, open to the page corresponding to the date of the tape. Off to one side, on a drafting table, he placed the chart or plotting sheet appropriate to each segment of the voyage. Thus he was able to collate log, chart and tape through nearly each nautical mile of *Hound's* passage, every tack, every course plotted and steered, every sail change and every word spoken by her skipper.

"*Fresh English sole for tea. Bought it from a fishmonger in Plymouth this morning. Sautéed it in butter and white wine. Perfectly dreadful! Tasted like bait marinated in diesel fuel.*"

(Break.)

"*Spectacular sunset! Aries steering vane working well. Have named it Amadeus. The purpose of this tape, patient listener, is to serve as a voice-over for a film I hope to make as soon as I discover how to operate my fucking ciné camera remotely. I have filmed the sunset and some clouds.*"

(Break.)

"*Six June. Lizard in the fog. Still dark. Just before first light. Can make out the loom. Hardened for the Scillies as wind veered a point. Seventy miles to go, then great circle for the Grand Banks!*"

(Pause.)

"*Hallo! Fog is gone. Just like that. I sailed right out of it. I can see the Lizard clearly now. And the morning stars. My God! There are dolphins both sides of the ship! Derdriu, you should see the phosphorescence in the water when a dolphin blasts by!*"

(Break.)

"*Egg, Irish bacon and soda bread for breakfast. Grand! Amadeus works whilst I wash.*"

(Break.)

*"Largish sail off to port. Think I've caught someone in Class A. One hundred forty miles noon to noon. Mad for this boat!"*

(Pause.)

*"Egg, Irish bacon and soda bread for lunch. Sleep required. None yet."*

(Break.)

Presumably he slept. There wasn't another entry for 6 June. Roger verified the early 6 June course change in the log and on the channel chart.

*"Seven June. Saw the Bishop's double flash off to port this morning as we cleared the Scillies. Wind is still southerly but going light and variable. Glass starting down . . . and there is a whiteness to the sky. Have decided not to shave."*

(Break.)

*"Wind has backed to the southeast."*

Roger turned off the tape recorder. Barbara, who had fallen asleep, was awakened by the silence. "Ow!" she said as her head nodded to one side, straining her neck.

"Storm coming," said Roger.

Chaim had sent a stack of surface weather maps for the period 5 June through the 28th, the span of *Hound's* participation in the race. There was a map of the entire North Atlantic for each day at twelve noon. Roger decided to trace the weather patterns along the OSTAR track and compare them with Con's experience. He dug out the map for 7 June. It showed a depression very near Con's noon DR for that day.

Barbara rubbed her neck and put on a pot of coffee. Roger restarted the machine.

*"Reefed main and rigged preventer. Flying now! Eight-point-five on steam gauge; ten surfing. Wind speed twenty-eight knots apparent."*

(Pause.)

*"BBC Shipping Forecast for Fasnet and Shannon: southerly gales Force eight to nine through tomorrow. Filled thermoses with soup and made packet of sandwiches with last of fresh bread. Think we're for it!"*

(Break.)

(Roaring in background with thumps and crashes at intervals.)

*"Blowing forty-five apparent. Double-reefed main and worker. Amadeus having trouble unless I flog the main. May need third reef. Noise on deck ... noise on deck is becoming infernal. Seas are probably twelve to fifteen feet although they seem twice that. I've read that one tends to overestimate the height of waves at sea. One is urged to multiply one's guess by 0.6."*

(Pause.)

*"Sights out of the question. Managed very shaky radio bearing on the Mizen Head, southwest Ireland."*

(Break.)

(High whine in background with thumps and crashes more frequent.)

*"Bare pole. Doing eight under bare pole. Heading nor'west. Rain squalls. Wind gusting to fifty. Seas look huge but are probably no more than twenty feet. Jaysus! I've never seen the like of this!"*

(Break. Tape keeps running but there is nothing more on it.)

Roger pulled out Chart 121 (North Atlantic Ocean, Northern Sheet) and spread it on the drafting table. He transferred Con's noon positions from the channel chart and plotting sheets to the big chart which covered the entire ocean. Roger did this so he could see the whole voyage on a single chart. Con's position on the eighth placed him sixty miles SSW of the Fasnet Rock. The RDF bearing on the Mizen Head was his last contact with Europe.

Roger reversed the tape, placed cassette #2, 9–15 June, in the machine and turned it on.

(The whine has subsided somewhat. Con's voice seems hoarse and strained. He utters three words, without emphasis.)

*"Nine ... June ... sleep."*

(Break.)

It was the only entry for 9 June.

(Break.)

*"Ten June. The worst is over. Force six now. From the north-*

west. Course two hundred fifteen mag under single-reefed main and number three."

(Pause.)

"It is . . . the bloody indifference of the sea which is so terrifying. And the wind's the same. No compromise. I can't say, 'Now wind, let's make a deal.' There are no deals. For the wind and the sea are not motivated by profit, nor by love, nor lust, nor flattery. But by pressure systems, for God's sake."

(Pause.)

"I was forward, capping the dorade ventilators. We were on the top of a following sea and were hurtling down the leeward face of what I perceived to be the ultimate wave. The wake created by the bow's headlong journey down the slope into that valley was like that of a naval destroyer. It came easily three feet above the deck. And when we struck the trough, the yacht continued down and the bow went right under. She must have broached then and been knocked down. For when I next saw daylight, the boat was lying on her side and I was in the water, connected to her only by a bit of three-eighths-inch Samson braid. I remember shouting. I shouted 'Please!' What a curious word to chose; neither expletive nor command. 'Please!' said I at the top of me lungs. But no one took any notice. In fact, another sea came along and I swallowed the half of it."

(Pause.)

"I've no idea how I got back aboard. However, had I not capped the ventilators, put in the companion slides and secured the cockpit lockers, my vessel should have filled and surely gone to the bottom. As it was, I lost the spinnaker topping lift block, somehow. Rig and hull are sound. However, I have injured the nail of my left thumb, which will involve some refingering."

(Break.)

"The ciné camera was a casualty of the gale. It flew across the main saloon like a bird but made a poor landing. Christ, it's cold with the wind northerly!"

(Break.)

"Eleven June. Four hundred eighty miles since noon on the seventh."

(Break.)

*"Tried to repair the ciné camera. Got so furious at the broken components, which are mostly plastic, that I flung the lot into the sea. So much for the Academy Award."*

(Break.)

*"Shall make stew laced with whisky for supper."*

(Break.)

*"Made whisky laced with stew!"*

(Chants noisily.)

*"Domine, non sum dignus! Domine, non sum dignus! . . ."*

(This trails off and he suddenly speaks in vaudeville Irish.)

*"Ah, Finn MacCunnaill!! Yew an' yer foin son, Oisín, would have shit yer buckskin britches in the tearin' tumult of gray mountain peaks of wahter Oiy beheld dese two days since!"*

(Pause.)

*"Will ye have a bit more stew, squire darlin'? Well . . . Oiy won't say no!"*

(Break. The break is followed by a remote English announcer's voice.)

*"This . . . is London."*

(A cheerful march, then the BBC time signal.)

*"Nineteen hundred hours. Greenwich Mean Time. And now the news."*

(Break. Con's voice.)

*"Bugger the news!"*

(Break. Then a velvety English woman's voice.)

*"We hear now the Concerto for Organ. Strings and Percussion by Francis Poulenc. The organist is Maurice Duruflé. Georges Prêtre conducts the French National Radio and Television Orchestra."*

(The music begins. And continues. It appears Con has taped the entire piece.)

Roger pressed the Fast Forward lever. The music appeared to fill the rest of the first side of the cassette and part of the second side. While Roger skipped through the tape, Barbara poured him a cup of coffee and allowed herself the new pleasure of leaving her hand on his shoulder.

(The music ends. Con's voice continues.)

*"Twelve June."*

(He's quite sociable.)

*"Crossed the full-powered channel-bound shipping lanes last night. Wind is southwest. Force three to four. We've been back to full main and number one since dawn. Calendar sunset now, with peach and purple clouds along the northern horizon. Ah Derdriu! The horizon, this evening, is full of grand castles and animals and faces of heroes and fine ladies."*

(Pause.)

*"Nor will it ever be seen by anyone exactly the same again."*

(Break.)

*"Thirteen June, latitude 51–20 north. Longitude 23–20 west. We are now west of Reykjavic, Iceland. Grand Marnier to celebrate."*

(Break.)

*"Barometer took a plunge; vast cover of cirrostratus approaching from the west, like an aircraft carrier upside-down. The moon is full . . . or nearly . . . with the most extravagant ring 'round it. Wind very light and starting to back."*

(Break.)

*"Bugger! Flat calm. Barometer down another half millibar. Slatting in the swell. Too fucking quiet."*

(Break.)

(There is a click, a pause, another couple of clicks, then chaos: the sudden, rasping, high whine of wind blowing across the standing rigging together with the deep tympanum sounds within the hull, and the noise of rushing water. Con shouts, sometimes incoherently.)

*"Fourteen June. . . . Full gale. . . . Started at dawn! The sight . . . of . . . this gray . . . wilderness under first light is . . . demoniac! . . . Wherever you look . . . from horizon to horizon . . . it is the same: the endless . . . outnumbering precipices and gulfs of the sea . . . some coming, some going . . . cliffs of water, curling and snarling . . . rising spreader high . . . then thundering by to crumble, with a roar, not a length away. Somehow . . . we stay just out of reach. . . . And the wind . . . my God . . . the wind*

*lacerates the face ... blows the tears from the eyes and the words from the ... "*

(There is a crash and a click then silence.)

"Is that the end of the tape?" Barbara asked.

"No, it's still running."

(The rest of the tape is blank.)

Roger removed the cassette. It was marked "9–15 June" but there was no entry for 15 June. Then Roger remembered. This was the same storm in which Captain Castaign had been obliged to heave-to in the eight-thousand-ton *Bearn*. If Con, in a five tonner, had made no entry on the fifteenth, it was understandable.

Roger transformed the 14 June noon position to the big chart and checked the weather map for the same day. He winced at what he saw. *Hound* had just entered an enormous depression, the most severe over the North Atlantic. The storm was huge; a great ugly swirl of isobars that looked like a bloated pistol target. It was 650 miles across, almost a hurricane. According to the map, the wind at Con's noon position was SSE at force ten (55–63 mph). And that was only the beginning. The wind would increase in velocity as *Hound* moved westward and the storm itself moved northeast. Understanding, as only a sailor can, the enormity of Con's predicament, Roger felt, for the first time since Newport, an ache of doubt.

Barbara saw it. She saw his eyes change; saw him swivel around in his desk chair and look out the window at the masts and rigging of the boats in the yard etched black against the sunrise. Some of the bow pulpits wore spider webs, like sequined shawls. Mossbunkers splashed in the basin. It was peaceful; so far from harm and the stormy sea. Barbara handed him Tape #3, 16–22 June.

"There's more," she said.

"He's a lot farther north than I expected him to be," Roger murmured. "It's possible he'll have to go over on starboard when he reaches the continental shelf." He stared out the window. "And, my God, in those conditions ..."

Barbara said softly, "Darling" (another first), "wait until

you've heard it all." She put the cassette in the machine and pressed the start lever.

(The voice, barely a whisper, is very Irish.)

*"I believe today is the sixteenth. Or perhaps the seventeenth. I don't know. For I have slept a long time. Probably it is the sixteenth."*

(Long pause.)

*"Now hear me, O'Dandy. . . . The boat saved me. In that tempest . . . that depravity, it was authentic bedlam. Lunacy. Without pattern or reason. The sea came from every direction. There was nothing I could do. Nothing, Desmond. I took off all sail, removed halyards that were not internal, removed the sheets and set the vane. After three, four, five hours, I gave in to it. I came below. I put in the slides, for what good it would do, came below and fell into the leeward bunk, oilskins, seaboots and all. I gave up. I slept . . . God only knows how long. And when I awoke, I thought I'd gone to heaven. For the sea was down. We were suspended in bright sunshine. And, from where I lay on the bunk, I could see a nimbus of light, reflected through one of the ports, which danced about on the overhead like an angel's smile. And, by some marvel of providence, the boat was still headed west.*

*"The boat did it, Desmond. The boat saved me. The boat enabled me to survive the same primal, natural forces, undiluted, which tested our forebears. . . . Conchobor. Cúchulainn and Macroth. Do you hear me, Desmond?"*

(He inhales slowly and sighs.)

*"Sure, the steel is harder now, after the annealing. And purer. And with a sharper cutting edge."*

(Break.)

(We hear the machine click on. There is a long pause. When Con speaks it is in an heroic, declamatory style.)

*"These are the javelins and shields and swords in the Téte Brec!*
*See for yourself!*

*The flickering of the gold sword-hilts and the*
                              *silver on the necks of javelins:*
*Conchobor's shield, Ochain,*
*The black shield Dubán belonging to Cúchulainn;*
*The bloody Croda,*
*The ringing shield of Sencha called Sciatharglan!*
*All in the Téte Brec!*
*See for yourself!"*


Roger snapped off the machine and looked at Barbara.

She shrugged. "What's he doing? Hallucinating?"

"I . . . don't think so," Roger said. "Des told me he and Con were raised with a firm hand and the Celtic epics at every meal. He said, in particular, that the deeds of a character named Cúchulainn had made a great impression on Con. Cúchulainn, by the way, was aka the Hound of Ulster."

"I remember. The professor objected to the name being used for the boat."

"That last bit sounded like a learned recitation . . . the sort of thing Damon would force Con to stand up and recite letter perfect or no dessert."

"But in the middle of the Atlantic. Isn't that a little flaky?"

"Maybe. What interests me more," Roger said, "is the heavy emphasis Con placed on the boat saving him. He addressed Des directly. 'The boat did it, Desmond. The boat saved me.' Didn't that sound . . . pointed, somehow? Urgent. As if he's trying to tell Des something particular."

"Like what?"

"I don't know. Any more coffee?"

"How about breakfast?" Barbara said, getting up and going over to the counter with the hotplate.

"Breakfast. Yes, please."

Barbara was not a breakfast eater. She rummaged through the cupboard and found some stuff Betsy had left.

"My dear, you have a choice this morning of Devil Dogs, Froot Loops or Fig Newtons."

"Coffee," Roger said and clicked the tape machine back on.

(Con's tape recorder is in the cockpit. The air over the mike makes a rasping sound.)

*"Seventeen June, I guess. Making good our westing now. Sea is moderate with a fine twelve-knot southerly. One hundred sixty miles noon to noon on two hundred eighty-four mag."*

(Break.)

*"Blast me for a clumsy idiot! I was on the foredeck with the Seapoint, trying to get a radio bearing, when a maverick wave heeled the yacht out of phase. I grabbed for the baby stay to keep from falling and lost the RDF over the side."*

Roger clicked the machine off, rewound and played back Con's last speech. He clicked off again.

"I think we finally have something," Roger said. Barbara came around and looked over his shoulder as he walked his dividers from Con's noon position on the seventeenth to the nearest land. The nearest land was the Avalon Peninsula of Newfoundland.

"Four, five, six, seven, seven-fifty," Roger counted, as he measured the distance. "Seven hundred fifty miles to the nearest radio beacon."

"Something wrong?"

"There isn't a radio beacon in the world, that I know of, with a range of over four hundred miles. And most of the coastal beacons in North America have ranges of one hundred miles." He pulled a paper bound book off the shelf behind the desk. It was *Radio Navigation Aids,* Pub. 117A, Atlantic and Mediterranean Sea. He found the page for Cape Race, Newfoundland.

"Look. Not one beacon in this part of Atlantic Canada with a range of over a hundred miles." He closed the book. "Con knows that as well as I do. I don't think he tried for a radio bearing seven hundred fifty miles out. I don't think he lost the RDF overboard, either. I think he made up the story to explain why it's missing. I think the real reason it's missing is that he took it with him when he went ashore."

Barbara stared. "When he went ashore? Roger, the life raft was still in the canister. Went ashore in what?"

"I don't know. Something. Have faith."

She smiled her sweet, full smile. "Oh, I do," she said. "I do."

They stopped then and went out to breakfast. Over poached eggs and sausage (he) and half an english muffin (she), they reviewed the past twelve hours.

"Well, it started superbly," Barbara said quietly, the soft blue eyes caressing his face. He grinned and shook his head in bewilderment.

"I 'uvoo," he said with his mouth full. He finished chewing and gasped. "I love you. I'm happy, Barbara. Happy!"

She reached across the table and took his hand. "Yes. You know who else is going to be happy?"

"Spencer."

"Yes."

"What about Betsy?"

"Absolutely. And since she's marrying Spencer anyway . . ." Roger's sudden frown stopped Barbara in midsentence. "What's the matter?"

"Mentioning Betsy reminded me of Derdriu which reminded me of Damon. When the old man wakes up he's going to call Des. Des still doesn't know the tapes have come down from St. Pierre. Unless he's completely innocent, I expect he'll be quite upset if he finds us poking through the log and listening to the tapes. After all, tapes like these are private, like letters."

"Oh," she said. "Isn't there a federal law about that?"

Roger glanced at his watch. "We have about two hours to get the cassettes and logbook back to Cath's. In the time left I think we should make copies."

They borrowed a Panasonic portable, bought some blank cassettes at Sandwich Radio and TV Repair, one of those village stores that is open at any hour if someone is home, and made a copy of the tapes starting with the gale of 14 June. During the taping, Barbara turned off the phone and photocopied the log. By nine o'clock they were up to the point where Con claimed he'd lost his RDF.

"Forward," said Roger. "We have an hour." He started the two tape machines.

(Con no longer dates his taped remarks. This apparently much later. He is subdued.)

*"What is the present day lucky for? It would soon be told if I had the gift. It would soon be told if I saw a maiden in a blue chariot drawn by two black horses. She has red hair in three tresses; auburn red like beech trees in fall: two wound round her head and the third hanging down her back, grazing her calves. Her eyebrows are black and arch above her gold-irised eyes, so lavishly lashed they cast shadows upon her cheeks. Her teeth are a finery of pearls set between lips of sage scarlet. She carries a light gold rod in one hand and a sword in the other. She is fresh from learning in Alba and has discovered the Light of Foresight. Her name is Fedelm, the Poetess of Connacht."*

Barbara gestured to Roger and he stopped the machine.

"That's the name Cath screamed," Barbara said. "Fedelm."

"Make a list of things to remember," he said. "We have to keep going."

(Tape #3 ends with Con in an hilarious mood. He shouts.)

*"He will be your Hound!*
*Guard all Murtheimne Plain*
*And Cúchulainn shall be his name!"*

*"Listen to the grand feats of the Hound of Ulster! The simplest first: to juggle nine apples with never more than one in the palm; the feats of the sword edge and the sloped shield, and the heroic salmon leap up the river's down water; the snapping mouth and the hero's scream; stepping on a lance in flight and straightening erect on its point; the feat of invisibility, performed within the concealing cloak of enchanted cloth woven by the witches of Tír Tairngire. And, lastly, the feat of the warp spasm in which his hair stands erect in a monstrous halo, he squeezes one eye narrower than the eye of a fly, opens the other wider than a trumpet bell and bares his jaws to the ear, peeling back his lips 'til the skull shows white!"*

(Con chuckles.)

113

*"Puts the wind up in the opponent, does that!"*
(Tape #3 ends.)

While Barbara rewound and set up for Tape #4, Roger transferred courses from the plotting sheets to the big North Atlantic chart. Con's 15 and 16 June positions, because of the gale, put him well north of the great circle track. On the seventeenth, however, there was a radical course change ... from 306 degrees to 284 degrees. This was the beginning of a new series of courses which would, presumably, clear Cape Race on the southeast corner of the Avalon Peninsula. The boat was still on port tack.

As Con had stopped dating his taped comments, Roger now relied solely on the log and charts for *Hound*'s daily positions as she approached the coast of Newfoundland. He verified Con's charted noon positions for the sixteenth, seventeenth, eighteenth, nineteenth, and twentieth. Then, abruptly, there were no more charted positions. The last position Con plotted on any chart was at noon on 20 June. It appeared in the extreme northeast corner of Canadian Grand Bank Chart No. 2666 ... the chart found on *Hound*'s chart table by Demonet and Lacombe. The position placed *Hound* 360 miles ENE of St. John's, two degrees north and a degree east of where she was sighted by *Bearn* eight days later. The logbook entry for 20 June matched: noon position 49–09N x 43–20W, course 276°.

On 21 June there was no charted position. However, Con's logbook for the twenty-first gave "Course 276, distance noon to noon 130 n.m." Roger took this information and lightly penciled in a 21 June position on the North Atlantic chart. He marked it "1200 DR, 6/21." *Hound* was now 230 miles or two days sail from St. John's.

Roger turned the page of the log. It was the last page in the book. It stated simply, "22 June, 1976. Course 276. Dist. noon to noon 135." This put *Hound* ninety-five miles from St. John's, less than a day's sail away. Beneath Con's last entry, toward the bottom of the page, were some notations. There were a few time and distance calculations, some figures subtracted for magnetic variation; nothing out of the ordinary. However, one doodle caught Roger's eye. Scribbled in the margin was

CSF CCCX ♪♩ ♪♩

Roger had no idea what it meant.

Barbara snapped Tape #4 into the machine. It was marked "23 June–     ."

The last log entry was on the twenty-second. Yet this tape was made on the twenty-third. That meant that Con was still aboard and sailing the day after he stopped writing up his log. It also meant that, sometime on the twenty-third of June, he was within sight of the coast of Newfoundland.

"We have a half hour," Barbara said.

"Press on," said Roger with growing excitement.

(Con's radio receiver is tuned to a pop music station. In the background, a girl is singing "Snowbird.")

*"I dreamed last night, Desmond. I dreamed of David Kean. It made me so cold I awoke and got into long johns and a balaclava."*

(Pause.)

*"Poor, dear Desmond. I've put you to such trouble, haven't I? Tell you what, Des! How about a holiday? Eh? A nice holiday in Avalon! A spot of hotel golf, eh? Take your mind off Leonetiac-macShitty!"*

(The girl singer finishes. An announcer gives the station break just as the radio is switched off. Con can be heard moving about. After quite a long interval he speaks. His voice trembles.)

*"And now, at last, I have about me the concealing cloak of Cúchulainn . . . woven from the enchanted cloth of Tír Tairngire. The blessed moment has come.*

> *"Desmond O'Dandy,*
> *Thy brother is dead;*
> *But hear what is writ*
> *On the foc's'l head:*

115

'Nay fishy swim
Near masty tang
Nor kelpy catch
On boomy-vang!
Wi' gate-valve fast
And garboard sound,
'Tis off, sweet curragh,
Brendan-bound!' "

(The rest of the tape is empty.)

# CHAPTER 17

"**P**oor Cath," whispered Cath as she gazed out the window of her room. Across a small, paved parking area she saw a kitchen ventilator whirling. The morning air already smelled of lunch.

"Why 'poor Cath'?" asked the young woman.

Cath sighed and closed her eyes. She was tired. She'd been talking for an hour. She longed to cry, to feel the cool, wet tears raining down her cheeks, comforting and commiserating. But she couldn't cry. She'd never been able to. The well was dry. The drill had failed to strike water. Against her parched lids, she saw a cracked, draught-stricken African landscape, covered with deflated imitation leather animals and pygmies, dead of thirst.

"Why 'poor Cath'?" the young woman repeated.

Cath opened her dry eyes and peered at the woman in the pale shirt dress and pearls. The shrinks didn't wear white coats in places like this. And the decor wasn't institutional. The emphasis here was on warmth and hominess. Like Howard Johnson's. It was supposed to reduce patient anxiety. With Cath it had the opposite effect. She looked past the flowered, slipcovered armchair in which the psychologist sat, to the print of Mystic Seaport on the wall. She shivered and wondered if the room was bugged and her movements monitored by a hidden TV camera. She looked at the young woman's waiting face.

"Poor Cath," she said. "Cath, who should have never grown into a woman at all. Cath, who should have remained twelve forever and always, running barefoot after sheep and dogs over the green velvet hills of Devon. Free as a boy. A child so . . . tender, so without malice she would have wept at the death of a moth had she been able."

She looked out the window again at the kitchen ventilator. "I remember her: a beautiful, slim child with pearl-white skin; long-waisted and lithe and full of joy and serenity . . . and love. Poor Cath. Poor Cath. If only the angels had broken the clock . . . sprinkled her with youth dust and confined her for eternity to age twelve."

She sighed and tried again to cry. After a moment she closed her eyes and lay back on her pillow. The psychologist waited.

"Would you like to sleep now?" the young woman said finally.

Cath nodded. The psychologist got up and tiptoed to the door. "There will be juice and cookies at ten in the family room," she said. "I hope it will be an opportunity for you to relax and try to make new friends."

The young woman left. A car went noisily past the window. Cath looked out and saw a white panel truck with "Conn. Uniform and Linen Supply" in red letters on its side. It was parked in front of the kitchen ventilator with its motor running.

Roger felt the first tug of exhaustion. He was going over the list Barbara had made. There were ten items; ten questions, actually, that had to be answered. Roger thought he already knew the answers to three. He checked these.

1. Who is Fedelm? (Damon to ask Des.)
2.   ″   ″   David Kean?
3. "Holiday in Avalon" probably Avalon Peninsula, Nfld. But what's "hotel golf"?
√4. "Leonetiac macShitty" = Celticism of Marshall Leonetti.
√5. "Concealing cloak of Cúchulainn" = FOG! (Roger had checked the surface weather map for 23 June. All the station models off the east coast of Newfoundland showed the characteristic symbol of three parallel lines that indicated thick fog. The "Concealing cloak," the fog, rendered Con invisible.)
6. "The blessed moment has come." Probably the moment when, close to shore in fog, Con abandoned *Hound* and homed on a radio beacon. (Which one?) Before he left the yacht he probably tacked her onto starboard and set the vane for the easterly course which finally brought her 350 miles east of St. John's and her meeting with *Bearn*.
√7. The poem to Des.

"Desmond O'Dandy,
Thy brother is dead;
But hear what is writ
On the foc's'l head:
Nay fishy swim
Near masty tang"   (*Mast tang*—fitting on mast to which shrouds holding mast are attached. No fish can swim near a mast tang unless the mast is under water.)

"Nor kelpy catch   (*Kelp*—type of seaweed.)
On boomy-vang!   (*Boom-vang*—tackle to regulate boom tension and mainsail shape.)

Wi' gate-valve fast   (*Gate-valve*—through hull fit-

119

ting to allow sea water in where needed. *Fast*—secured.)

And garboard sound,

(*Garboard*—last plank before keel in wood boat; vulnerable. *Sound*—undamaged, strong.)

'Tis off, sweet curragh,

(*Curragh*—traditional Irish skin boat.)

Brendan-bound!"

(*Brendan*—Irish saint alleged to have sailed the ocean to America in the ninth century.)

Roger concluded, from the doggerel, that Con was supposed to sink the boat. All he had to do was open a gate valve or chop through the hull at the "garboard," the boat would go down like a stone and Leonetti would have his hundred thousand back plus another hundred. But Con apparently couldn't do it. After the gale of 14 June, Con says, "Now hear me, O'Dandy . . . the boat saved me . . . the boat did it, Desmond." By not sinking the boat, Con double-crossed Leonetti.

The last questions on the list were

8. What is CSF CCCX ♪·♪ ♪♪ in logbook?
9. How did Con get ashore?
10. Where is Con now?

Roger, heavy with fatigue, put the list to one side and called Spencer. "Will you run the yard for a few hours while I grab some sleep on the schooner?"

"Certainly," Spencer said. "By the way, do I or do I not detect a new and happy gleam in your eye?"

"Yes," Roger said. "I love her. I want to marry her."

There was a silence. Spencer cleared his throat. "I have never," he said, "had better news."

Barbara took the tapes and logbook back to Cath's house before ten. The girls were up preparing Damon's breakfast. The kitchen was tidy and businesslike and Barbara noticed both girls wearing dresses and half aprons instead of the usual shorts and

T-shirts. While Barbara sipped a cup of tea, Damon came down. Here, too, was a change. Damon was freshly showered and shaved and wore a fine old Irish-linen suit with a floppy bow tie.

"Like Synge," he said. "Well, there's work to be done. My keepers have declared with some emphasis that a new decorum shall prevail in this household . . . an outward and physical embellishment, to be sure, of an inward and spiritual determination. Ah! Bangers for breakfast!"

"Ten more minutes for the bangers, Granddad," said Derdriu. "But here's your tea."

"I'll call Desmond, then," he said, taking his tea to the kitchen phone.

Des had arranged for a charter airplane to take Michele Parinello, her mother and himself to Block Island for the weekend. He felt ridiculous. Michele was eighteen. She was the new secretary at Macroth, Jane Pond's replacement. She was a cousin of Marshall Leonetti's wife, a Catholic and a brickyard, body and fender Venus of unimaginable voluptuousness who would not, repeat, would not put out. Des was frantic. He imagined he was developing bladder trouble. Michele's mother, Gloria, looked more like Michele's older sister than her mother, except for the hairdo, a teased stack of curls, buns and rats which resembled the temples at Angkor Wat.

Des was packing a Land's End duffle while the two women, wearing matching running shorts, Adidas and tank tops, did their nails and watched a morning game show on TV. The phone rang.

"Hallo?"

"Who's Fedelm?" said Damon.

"Is that you, Father?"

"The same."

"What'd you ask?"

"Who's Fedelm?"

"Is this a morning quiz?" Des looked over at the two women watching TV and had the idiotic sensation that he was on the show himself.

121

"Desmond, who is Fedelm?" the old man asked again.

"Why, the poetess of Connacht who foretold Cúchulainn's victory at Murtheimne."

"No, you dimwit, who is Fedelm to Cath? Why would the name drive Cath wild?"

Des took a deep breath and held it. Surely it was fifteen years ago. Maybe more. He saw the tall, handsome, red-haired, black-eyed dancer, holding a Brownie camera and standing on the cliffs over the narrows into St. John's harbor, the gulls soaring behind her on the updrafts and the wind whipping her skirt above the curve of her thighs.

"Why do you ask, Father?"

"Never mind. Come at once."

"I have weekend plans, Father. I'm to leave within the hour."

The old man's intonation dropped menacingly. "You'll not," he growled. "You'll do as you're told." Des felt a vestigial boyhood fear at the sound of that voice, so filled with the promise of punishment. He looked longingly at Michele who was regarding him sideways from beneath a black hedge of lashes.

"Can't it wait until Monday, Father?"

"Who's David Kean?" Damon asked.

An almost uncontrollable urge to resign flowed through Des at that moment. He longed for the peace and silence of surrender, so much sweeter than the struggle. Nevertheless, his automatic defense apparatus went off, like a sprinkler system. Alarm bells rang at this danger of compliance.

"I'll come, Father."

In spite of Derdriu's new accountability, Barbara decided it was too soon for her to hear her father's voice on tape. So, before Des arrived, Barbara reminded Derd that Ernie Hall needed bluefish bait and was paying the kids two cents apiece for mossbunkers. The girls changed their clothes and went off.

"Incredible!" said Des solemnly when Damon turned off the final tape. He shook his head and chug-a-lugged his second martini. "Incredible that Con should remember those sections of *The*

*Táin* after all these years! And references to the Fenian and Ulster cycles as well. Aren't you impressed, Father?"

Damon grunted and focused on his second son.

"Well, Desmond?"

Des got up to make another drink. Walking across the room to the liquor cabinet, he made a great effort to present the exterior of a man deeply moved by his dead brother's last words while sorting out the jumble within. The tapes! The fucking tapes! He'd nearly forgotten about them. How the hell did they get sent to Cath? He forced his mind back to that foggy night in St. Pierre. Roger Truly. Roger must've given the little Frenchman Cath's address. Des wondered if that was a tactical move on Roger's part or innocence. He decided to assume tactical. Better judge Roger suspect. And his girl too. God! What an ass Con was to make that last tape! "Desmond O'Dandy, thy brother is dead." Asshole!

He smiled at Barbara from the liquor cabinet. She had, he noticed, become excessively attractive; enough to be annoying.

"Can I get you something?"

"What time is it?" Barbara asked.

Des glanced at his watch. "Half after twelve."

"A perfect Rob Roy straight up with a twist," she said demurely.

"Father?"

"Not now," growled the old man. "Well, Desmond? Come on, then. What about Fedelm?"

Des cracked ice. "Fedelm," he murmured. "Fedelm was . . . is . . . Cath Macroth's nemesis. It's difficult to grasp after all these years. Fedelm is Cath's bête noir." He stirred Barbara's drink in the mixer. "Father, there's nothing mysterious about this. Fedelm's real name is Moira O'Leary . . . from St. John's. She was a dancer: tall and handsome with long, beautiful legs. Like the legendary Fedelm, she'd flaming auburn hair to the backs of her knees and black eyes. Con had an affair with her before he married Cath. But what upset and, apparently, still upsets Cath, happened one midsummer's eve. My God, it's years ago!" He poured Barbara's drink and took it to her.

"Cath and Con were on holiday near St. John's. Cath, for no discernible reason, went into one of her depressions. Con was used to it. He administered pills, put her to bed and let her sleep it off. As I said, it was midsummer's eve, a traditional time for Celtic hijinks. Well. Con drove into St. John's and found Moira. They had some drinks. Eventually, with the mischief in them, they drove to a country club and lit ritual bonfires on the golf course." Des poured his martini. "At some point in the evening, Moira took off most or all of her clothes and Con painted her body blue. In the flickering light of the bonfire, she resembled a Celtic Druidess, or so it said in the newspapers. Con told the reporters that Moira was Fedelm, poetess of Connacht, she of the sage red lips and the Light of Foresight. As a result, she became a minor celebrity in St. John's. For awhile. And, of course, the name stuck.

"She never really meant much to Con; only that she was everything Cath was not: tall, mischievous and sexy. Fedelm is not the problem, Father. Cath is the problem. Cath has been paranoid about the woman all her married life. If Con went to the grocery store and was ten minutes' overdue, she was absolutely certain he'd fled to St. John's to be with Fedelm." Des sipped his drink and returned to the chair next to his father.

"As for Deavid Kean ... you must remember him, Da. He lived in St. Catherine's Street, Belfast. He was only a wee chap. Died of tuberculosis before the war. He couldn't have been more than ten. Actually, we wouldn't have remembered him at all, only it was our first experience of death." Des paused and looked directly at his father. "When Con said 'I dreamed of David Kean and it made me cold,' he may have been anticipating his own death."

Damon looked out the window and scratched his ear. "I thought it was Gordy Sullivan died of tb."

"No father. David Kean."

The phone rang. Barbara answered. It was Doctor Comstock. "Mrs. Macroth has disappeared from the psychiatric facility," he said. "She stole a laundry truck. They found it on the junior-high-school baseball diamond. Has she turned up at home?"

"No."

"Well, I'm afraid we'll have to notify the police."

"Off to St. John's, I'm sure," said Des cheerfully when he heard the news. He allowed his spaniel eyes to travel over Barbara. "Another Rob Roy?"

"No thanks. I've got to get back to the yard."

"Let me drop you."

"No thanks. I'd rather walk." Barbara left. She went out the kitchen door and through the garage. She was certain Cath's MG had been parked in the driveway when she came in.

On her desk at the office, Barbara found a sealed envelope marked "B. F." It contained a note, a front door key and a check for two hundred dollars.

Barbara dear: One last favor. Please look after Derd and Damon for a week or so. And open any mail that seems important. Must do this. Gratefully, Cath.

# CHAPTER 18

The police waited for Cath at Bradley International and Logan. She never appeared.

"They're wasting their time," Derdriu said, nibbling a fingernail. "She won't fly. She'll drive. It'll take days."

The Massachusetts, New Hampshire and Maine State Police were notified. So were U.S. Customs and Immigration at Portland and Bar Harbor and Canadian Customs at Yarmouth. None of them ever saw the dark green MG with the Connecticut plate "Cath-1."

"She may be daft," Derdriu said, "but she's not dumb. There are tons of ways of getting into Canada without going through Customs."

"Try not to worry, Derd," Barbara said.

"Sure, it's not her I'm worried about," the child said.

Just before lunch on Sunday, *Yardbird* chugged into the basin with *Hound of Ulster* in tow. Griff and Bryan hadn't slept for twenty-four hours. Roger rafted both boats at the rigging dock and sent the two men home to bed. Later, he and Spencer sculled *Hound* over to her old slip. When she was secure, Roger phoned Art Scholfield, the surveyor, and made an appointment for him to come down next morning to survey *Hound* for the insurers.

Barbara had spent the morning with Derd and Betsy, making household lists and satisfying herself they understood the dishwasher, the washing machine and when to put out the garbage. She could have saved herself the trouble.

"They've got everything under control," she said as Roger and Spencer came into the office for lunch. "All I have to do is dole out the petty cash and take care of Cath's mail."

Roger and Spencer sat with Barbara on the roof and dined on chef's salad.

"I wish," said Spencer, stabbing pieces of ham and cheese, "we knew how the hell Con got ashore... assuming he did. Because, until we do, we can't really be certain he's alive." Spencer worked on an anchovy. "And, my friends, I submit the following with utmost affection and a desire to be helpful: you've based your calculations of Con's landfall on *his* courses, *his* distances and *his* dates. Isn't that right?"

"Right," said Roger.

"Yet you said yourself, if he could fake the trial he could fake the rest. How can you be sure he didn't fake the log and the tapes, that the courses plotted are not the courses he steered and that he simply invented the dates?"

"We can't," Roger said. "At least, not yet."

Next morning at eight, Art Scholfield went to work on *Hound*. He finished the survey in a little over three hours and came up to the office with his clipboard. Roger sat at the desk.

"Christ, Roger, she's a corker! Who built her? Mattel? They used automobile putty to fair her topsides. And the way the house is fastened I wouldn't put up a pantry shelf. Still, what's there is sound enough, I guess. There's some crazing in the way of the port chainplate which ought to be corrected and she's tin-canned forward: prob'ly ought to have two bilge stringers instead of one.

"What's she worth?" Roger asked.

Scholfield grunted and looked at the ceiling. "'Bout twenty, I should imagine."

"Spencer'll be glad to hear that. The surveyor for the salvors figures twenty-eight."

"You fellas hash it out. I'll have this written up by tomorrow if Elinor got the new ribbon for the Underwood. Well. We'll see ya, Roger. Have a nice day." He started out, stopped with the screen door half open and came back. He lowered his voice. "I'm not supposed to ask this, but are the owners going to keep her equipment or auction it off?"

"There isn't any equipment, you old bandit." Roger laughed. "She was vandalized."

Scholfield looked chagrined. "Pity," he said. "I woulda bid on the Avon."

Roger stared at him. "Avon? What Avon?"

"Christ, Roj, I dunno. I found the foot-pump bag aboard."

Roger got up. "Where?"

"In the starboard dorade box. I pulled off the vent to check the baffles and it was stuffed right in there. Looked brand new."

Roger felt his heart thump. "Show me," he said.

They left the office and headed for *Hound*'s slip.

"I think there was a kicker aboard, too," Art said as they trotted across the yard. "There's a slick of outboard fuel in the engine bed. Prob'ly a Seagull or something, stowed in there on its side. Them little outboard carburetors all leak some. God, Roger! What's your hurry?"

They reached the boat and went aboard. Art handed Roger the bag. It looked like a cheap cloth bag with a puckerstring. Actually it was made of crossgrained paper and had a waxy, semiwaterproof exterior. There was no mistaking it. It was the disposable white bag the Avon company used to pack the foot bellows for their Redstart and Redcrest inflatable dinghies. There would be no reason to have the bag aboard without the bellows and no reason for the bellows without the dinghy.

They went below. Behind the companion ladder and between the stringers of the engine bed, were rust marks from cans that had been stowed there. Art moved the beam of his flashlight aft of the rust marks and Roger saw the small, shiny puddle. He reached out, rubbed his finger in it and sniffed. The smell was gasoline and the residue on his finger oil. Oil and gas mixed. Outboard fuel.

That evening, Cliff Leonard sat on the office sofa with his bulging old strap and buckle briefcase by his side. The insurance investigator had come up from New York at Spencer's bidding. ("Cliff, we got the bastards right by the goddam short hairs!") With Barbara and Spencer flanking him on the couch, he listened politely to Roger's presentation.

"There is no way we can prove conclusively that he steered the courses he plotted or traveled the distances he logged," Roger said, glancing at his notes. "However, I don't think we need proof as there is other evidence which supports the fact that, on the twenty-third of June, he was less than twenty miles off the Avalon Peninsula.

"First, we have established beyond doubt it was the twenty-third. You'll recall, on Con's final tape, a girl was singing a pop song in the background. After her song there was a station break. The *Bearn* depositions stated that, when *Hound* was boarded, her radio was in good working order and tuned to station CKZN, St. John's. If you listen carefully to the tape you can hear those call letters. This morning, Barbara phoned the station and found the song "Snowbird," sung by Ann Murray, was played at four-seventeen P.M. on the twenty-third and has only been played once since . . . on two July. Thus we have established the time he abandoned the yacht. It was between four and five P.M. on Wednesday, twenty-three June.

"Using the footbellows included with every dinghy, Con inflated the Avon on the boat's largest open space, the foredeck.

Instead of pitching the bellows bag over the side, which would be unthinkable to most sailors, Con stowed it in the starboard dorade vent, the way one would a winch handle. He launched the inflatable, clamped on the motor, put the foot pump aboard, extra fuel, a few clothes, his Radio Directional Finder and the chart of Conception Bay. He may have taken his sextant or ditched it. Certainly he wouldn't have needed it in the fog. We believe the empty sextant box was planted deliberately to give the impression he was lost overboard taking a sight."

Cliff Leonard cleared his throat. His pince-nez threw sparklers. "How do you know he took the chart of Conception Bay with him?"

"Because," said Roger, "we ordered his charts through New York Nautical and Canadian Hydrographic. We have a list. The Conception Bay chart is the only one missing."

Cliff nodded.

"With the inflatable alongside, he brought the yacht about and set the vane to steer a course of about 123 degrees magnetic or 095 degrees true. There was a light southerly blowing. He'd already tied in a reef and put on the working jib in case of heavier weather later. She was probably sailing herself east at three or four knots when he went into the dinghy, undetected from shore or elsewhere, by the 'Concealing cloak of Cúchulainn!' . . . the thick Grand Banks fog.

"We always assumed Con was headed for St. John's. It's the center of everything on the peninsula. Actually, it's the last place he would've wanted to go. If he'd succeeded in getting ashore there without being seen, he'd have had other difficulties . . . getting rid of the dinghy and motor, for instance. As our projection of his course on the twenty-third shows, he was some twenty miles north of St. John's by five P.M. When we discovered the Conception Bay chart was missing, we realized he'd headed not for St. John's but for the entrance to Conception Bay, Cape St. Francis. Which explains the cryptic notation on the last page of the log."

Roger showed Cliff a photocopy of the scribble

# CSF CCCX ♪ ♪

"CSF is the abbreviation for Cape St. Francis Light. CCCX is the Roman numberal for 310, the radio beacon's frequency. And, thanks to Barbara's music lessons long ago, we know that a dotted eighth note and a sixteenth, repeated, is the same as dash-dot, dash-dot. The radio beacon appears, along with Cape Race and Cape Spear, on page 12 of Publication 117-A, Radio Aids to Navigation, Atlantic." He showed Cliff the page.

"Cape St. Francis, Freq 310, Char-.-. (3 times) Gp Seq III, Range 100."

"Con simply tuned his RDF to 310 kHz and homed on the beacon until he could see the lighthouse. Then he altered course and rounded the cape into Conception Bay."

Roger put the volume back on the desk. "This leaves 'hotel golf' as the next-to-last item on our list. When we heard Con say to Des 'How about a holiday in Avalon—a spot of hotel golf?' it sounded fairly natural. At first. I visualized an old summer hotel with a putting green attached. Then Barbara listened to the tape again and realized that hotel and golf were the international code words for the letters H and G; that perhaps H and G stood for something. We looked at the Sailing Directions for Newfoundland-Labrador and noted the names of the principal ports in Conception Bay. They are Wabana, Topsail, Holyrood, Brigus, Bay Roberts, Carbonear and Harbour Grace.

"We think he might've taken the Avon into Harbour Grace—it's only twenty miles from Cape St. Francis—and ditched it on a remote part of the northern shore, east of the town. If we're right, it's likely the dinghy and motor were or will be salvaged. We're waiting to hear from Angus MacIvor. He's making inquiries among the fishermen."

Roger put his notes away. "The final and most difficult question, of course, is where is Con Macroth now? While there is no way we can be sure, we think we have a lead worth following. Con's wife is, at this moment, on her way to St. John's by car."

Cliff frowned. "Driving to St. John's, Newfoundland? Why?"

"She's convinced Con is alive and consorting with another woman there. Her convictions must be pretty strong. St. John's is a four- or five-day trip from here by road and automobile ferry. She's driving because she's afraid to fly."

"Roger," said Cliff, "are you saying that Macroth deliberately staged this drama so he could walk into the sunset with another woman?"

"No. What I'm saying is that his wife is sure enough he's in St. John's to venture a fifteen-hundred-mile trip, alone, in an MG."

Spencer interrupted. "Roger, while I'm entirely on your side, I think you should mention that Cath broke out of the local laughing academy to make this voyage."

Roger nodded. "I know that. She's a crafty lady. Nevertheless I have a strong hunch she'll eventually lead us to Con." He turned to Cliff. "There's still time to pick up her trail. She has to take the automobile ferry from Sydney to Argentia, Newfoundland. Cliff, all you have to do is station a man at the Argentia ferry slip. When she drives off he follows her. Simple as that."

There was no response. Roger walked to the office refrigerator. "Well," he sighed, "I've spoke my piece. Another beer, Cliff?"

Cliff sat still for a moment. He wore a melancholy expression on top of a half smile. Finally, he shook his head. His glasses wiggled.

"No more beer, thanks," he said. He placed his old briefcase on his lap. "Roger. It's a good yarn. I take it that what you hope for is a full-scale insurance investigation based on your . . . um . . . conclusions?"

"Yes."

The melancholy expression deepened. "I can't recommend it," Cliff said sadly.

Spencer jumped up and waved his arms. "What in blazes do you want, you old lizard? It's cut and dried! He's giving you the son of a bitch on a paddle!"

"Spencer," Cliff said quietly, "my client is a big company. He got that way by not throwing good money after bad. Don't be

132

offended. I think Roger and Barbara have uncovered a great many fascinating details. But I cannot recommend a full-scale investigation on the basis of allegations. Roger keeps saying 'We think' and 'Maybe.' I have to have hard evidence before I can proceed. Facts. The yacht was found abandoned on June twenty-eighth by a French cargo vessel. That's a fact. She was brought to New York as a salvage prize on July seventeenth. Also a fact. There were indications she'd been vandalized ... although nobody saw it happen. Con Macroth may have had an inflatable dinghy. Nobody has seen it. He may have homed on St. Francis radio beacon. He may have gone ashore at Harbour Grace and his wife may know where he is now. Nobody really knows. And, Spencer, until somebody really knows something, I can't request funds, make a budget and send men to Canada."

"Then I'll go," said Roger.

"We'll go," Barbara said.

Cliff regarded Roger sympathetically. He looked around at the disappointed faces. Finally he unlocked his briefcase.

"All right," he said gently. "It's a long shot. A very long shot. But, if your hunches are right and you are determined to go up there at your own expense and try to find him, you'd better be prepared for a few surprises." Cliff rummaged through the old briefcase. "If he's alive, you can be sure he's altered his identity and probably his physiognomy. You will be looking for a man whose face you no longer know. Further, in spite of his wife's convictions to the contrary, he's probably left Newfoundland. A man on the run usually picks the biggest city he can find, where imposters are a dime a dozen and half the population goes incognito."

Cliff found what he was looking for. He withdrew a battered pamphlet from the briefcase and handed it to Roger. It was an old Department of Justice publication entitled "Criminal Use of False Identification."

"Take this with you and study it carefully," he said. "It might save you time."

He buckled his briefcase and got up. He nodded to Barbara and offered his hand to Roger. "I wish you both the very best of luck," he said, gravely. "But if, by some miracle, you find, him, promise me this . . ."

Roger and Barbara listened solemnly.

"Promise me you won't try to take him; promise that, wherever you are, you will call Egality's 800 number and let us contact the Royal Canadian Mounted Police."

"We promise," Roger said.

# PART FOUR

# DAVID KEAN

# CHAPTER 19

"Tuesday, 20 July," Barbara wrote in her journal. "There are a number of things I have never understood. One of them is time. Why, for instance, is Newfoundland time an hour and a half later than Connecticut time? I put this burning question to Roger on the plane. But he explained it to me with such patient condescension that I stopped listening almost immediately and now don't give a shit.

"Spencer, bless him, is taking care of Cath's mail and denmothering Damon and girls 'til we get back. Am writing this in front seat of mulberry Vega rented at St. John's airport. Roger's idea: go straight to Argentia, meet Cath coming off ferry."

— ✻ —

The adventure started badly. St. John's to Argentia, by road is about a hundred miles, most of it via the Trans-Canada Highway. But Roger took a shortcut.

"Never," Barbara wrote later, "take shortcut in Newfoundland without bread and water."

The Vega bounced and bucked over a washboard dirt-and-gravel track that wandered through treeless, pond-dotted bracken for forty miles. They were slowed once by fog near the coast. When it cleared, Roger drove too fast and broke a shock. He nearly hit a moose. When they finally limped into Argentia at dusk, the ferry had come and gone. Roger squealed to a stop near the Canadian National wharf, ran down the ramp, vaulted the gate and glared at the empty slip. It was an arrogant and futile gesture.

"He's obsessed," Barbara wrote. "Thinks he knows where gold is buried. Never seen him like this."

They called the CN office for the ferry schedule and to inquire if Cath had been aboard the last vessel. She had not. The next boat was due at eight A.M. the following morning. Nothing to do but wait.

They checked into the only rooms left in town: O'Dougherty's Hospitality House. Roger bunked with an Icelandic fisheries inspector and a paint salesman from Toronto. Barbara would share a room with Mrs. O'Dougherty's daughter as soon as a cot could be brought up from the cellar. While this was being attended to, Barbara called Sandwich. Spencer answered.

"I'm goddam glad you called," he said. "The old perfesser and I have become pretty good buddies but Betsy and Derdriu have had a falling out."

"Why?"

"Dunno. Derdriu's spending the night with her uncle."

"With Des?"

"Yes. Want to speak to Betsy?"

"Please."

Barbara listened while Spencer called her daughter. She could hear Betsy's footsteps hurrying down the stairs.

"Mom?"

"Hi."

Betsy was on the edge of tears. "Mom, it's really the pits here. I want to go back to the apartment."

"What's wrong, honey?"

Betsy let out a sob. "It's Derd. She's all pissed off because you're up there looking for her father. She says you guys should mind your own damn business. She says I'm not her friend anymore. And she says you're shacking up with Roger? Is that true?"

The village of North Isle is on the Maine–New Brunswick border between Grand Lake and Houlton. The entrance to the tiny North Isle public library is in the United States while its parking lot is in Canada. Both Canadians and Americans use the library daily and come and go as they please. It was here that Cath slipped across the border unnoticed. She drove through Fredericton, Moncton and into Nova Scotia at Amherst. She reached the ferry dock in Sydney Wednesday night, the night Roger and Barbara drove into Argentia.

In four days and twelve hundred miles she never faltered, never took a wrong turn, never exceeded the speed limit and never slept for more than an hour. Her only discomfort came from a recurring fantasy: Con is naked on his back, spread-eagled, his arms over his head; Fedelm, the dancer, the giantess, naked, red hair to her waist, breasts full standing, nipples erect, lowers herself in a split above his swollen phallus. She suspends herself there for a moment, teasing. Then, with a shriek of lewd laughter she lowers herself onto him, burying his organ within her. She shrieks with delight, rises slowly, gasps, lowers herself again. She moans and begins to rotate. Faster. She pivots and rotates. Faster. Enraptured, on the edge of her ecstasy, she throws back her head and screams "Now!"

"Now," Cath says, and fires.

The fantasy always left Cath tense and aroused. She was ashamed of this feeling and fought against it. But once, in New Brunswick, it got the better of her. She pulled off the road and tried to masturbate. She closed her eyes and made an effort to materialize Con's mouth. It wouldn't materialize. After some unsuccessful moments, she gave up, put her head on the back of the seat and tried to relax. Almost immediately she had the feeling she was being watched. She opened her eyes and looked out the car window into the benign face of a Guernsey cow. The ludicrousness of the situation swept her mind clean for awhile. But eventually the fantasy returned.

Once, Derdriu was involved. Not really involved. Just there. Watching. It disgusted Cath and fed her feelings of betrayal by her daughter.

Derd was her father's child. Since she was tiny, Con had romanced her: with Celtic tales of grandeur, with preposterous adventure stories in which Derdriu was the protagonist, with sailing stories and sagas of the sea. And with music. Cath hated music. She couldn't carry a tune. She couldn't distinguish a musical phrase, emotionally or cerebrally. It made her feel deprived and angry. She knew horses, houses, flowers and clothes. She could put them into perspective and make a qualitative judgment. But the Emperor Concerto and "Fly the friendly skies of United" were all the same to her.

Once, when Derd was about three, she awoke in the night, weeping. Con got up. Cath remembered lying alone in bed, trembling with frustration as Con cradled their daughter in his arms, carried her downstairs to the piano and, with her on his lap, softly played and sang her to sleep.

> "My little girl
> Pink and white as peaches and cream
> Is she . . ."

The pied-viper, Cath thought. Softly, siren-singing her child away.

Roger listened to the Icelander discuss the deterioration of the Newfoundland fishery. Mrs. O'Dougherty interrupted. "Dey have your party in St. John's sor," she said. Roger hurried down the stairs and picked up the hall phone.

"Angus?"

"Hallo, Roger. Had ye a good flight tew our elegant oisle?"

"Yes, thank you Angus. Any news of the dinghy?"

Angus cleared his throat. "Yis and no, Roger." He lowered his voice importantly. "Nothin' whatever was found in Harbour Grace, Roger. Oiy have a cousin there was the soul of a larcenist. He combed every inch of the north and south shore of Harbour Grace from Ship Head Loight to Feather Point. Dere was no sign of yer dinghy, Roger. But, yisterday, Oiy run into Tommy Dolan from Portugal Cove."

"Yes?"

"Portugal Cove is on t'other side of the Bay from Harbour Grace, Roger. Oh, It'll be twenty-five or turty miles mebbe across the Bay from Harbour Grace and in behind Bell Oisland."

"Did this guy find the dinghy?"

"No. But last week his son come home from mackerelin' wit a five-horsepower Seagull outboard motor in t'bottom of t'skiff. Now Roger, dem don't grow on trees in Newf'n'land."

"I know," said Roger. "Please continue."

"Well. Mick Dolan ... dat's Tom's boy ... was fishin' dem inlets between Bell Oisland and Cape St. Francis. About five mile below t'cape, dere's an inlet named Puffin Cove. Mick come into t'cove for mackerel at low tide when he spied an outboard motor lyin' ont'shingle deep in t'bight of t'cove. De motor was half submerged. Now Roger, dat shingle is really a small oisland of loose rock. So Mick went round t'backside and beached t'skiff outa t'surge. He come ashore, then, an' seen t'outboard motor was clamped to the ass end of an inflatable dinghy."

Roger was elated. "Super, Angus! Was there anything left in the dinghy?"

Angus allowed his voice to become prophetic. "No, Roger. Dere was nuttin' left *in* t'dinghy." He paused for emphasis. "An' dere was nuttin' left *of* t'dinghy neither. Mick said she'd been sliced by a ship's propeller."

Roger had a sudden, sickening picture of Con Macroth run down in the fog just miles from his destination; dead, bloated, floating face up just below the surface of the sea.

"Thanks, Angus," Roger said. "I'll call when we get back to St. John's."

Cath was first in line at the CN East Coast Marine and Ferry. The boat would leave at two P.M. the next day. She sat in the MG for fourteen hours, getting out only once to go to the bathroom and buy her ticket. She neither slept nor ate but sat very still, controlling her anger. She stared at an ad for Molson's Beer plastered on a brick wall opposite her parking spot and thought of Con and his redheaded whore.

Boarding started at noon. Cath drove the MG down a small service road, up a steel ramp and through the open jaws of the ferry into a vast cavern. It stank of carbon monoxide. She drove to the farthest corner of the cave and parked. The car was secured and she was directed to her cabin on an upper deck. The cabin was small but airy. It had its own washstand and mirror but no toilet. Though the accommodation was meant for two, Cath was the sole occupant. She stripped to her underwear, washed in the basin, brushed her teeth and turned down the lower berth. She took the Baretta from an overnight bag and the .22 caliber ammunition from an aspirin bottle in her purse. She loaded the clip carefully, inserted it, pushed the safety catch and placed the gun under her pillow. Then she climbed into bed and fell asleep almost immediately.

# CHAPTER 20

Des awoke at daybreak. He was in a foul mood. It was hot. He hadn't slept. He was frightened and angry and beset by a feeling of helplessness that seemed to manifest itself in leg cramps. He longed for a drink. But it was too early, even for him. He got up, put on sweatpants, a sweatshirt and the new Pumas Gloria had made him buy. He wrapped a towel around his neck and quietly let himself out into the sweltering morning. He reckoned Derdriu would sleep another hour.

He started to run. He ran until the sweat ran down his body, down his legs into his socks. He ran until the cramps were gone, until his mind cleared and the fear and anger subsided. After three miles he reached a decision about Roger Truly, turned around and jogged home. It was nearly seven o'clock when he got back to the house. He realized he was starved for eggs and bacon and strong Irish tea with milk.

The ferry *Cabot Strait* passed Isaac Point. When the Argentia harbor buoy opened up to starboard, her skipper rang for All Ahead Slow and began his wide turn. He warped her at 0840 and, twenty minutes later, started offloading. Cath was first ashore. She spun her wheels on the slippery upgrade and flashed through the gate. Roger, still upset at the news of the torn Avon, nearly missed her. He gunned the Vega just in time.

Cath seemed to know exactly where to go. Roger and Barbara followed her north for a little over an hour then onto the Trans-Canada east. Just before noon, they entered St. John's. The city streets seemed to have no pattern but ran up and down hill, formed crescents and circles and changed names in the middle. Cath never faltered. She turned off Queen's Road, drove down a tiny cobbled alley lined with brown and gray clapboard houses, emerged onto Duckworth, negotiated a tortuous detour onto a potholed secondary road, shifted down and, after a long climb in low gear, turned off into the parking lot of the Signal Hill Hotel. The rambling two-story building was perched on the edge of a precipice seven hundred feet above St. John's harbor. From it the view was staggering.

To the southwest lay the harbor, sparkling in natural splendor beneath a pale midday sun. But packed along every foot of its perimeter were the rude paraphernalia of hard maritime mercantilism. Nearly everything on the peninsula came and went by ship. The harborside was jammed with ships: tankers, dry cargo ships, container ships, coasters and freighters; pilot boats, tugboats, fishing boats and barges. And over them brooded the dark, watchful twin-spired Catholic church. To the southeast, through the Narrows (which seemed a slit hacked through a mountain), lay Cape Spear, the easternmost point in North America, closer in sea miles to Galway than to Washington, D.C.

Roger parked the Vega next to a camper from Quebec and got out. He wasn't prepared for the wind. It nearly tore the car door

144

off. He braced himself and watched Cath struggle across the parking lot to the hotel entrance. The entrance and the lobby behind it were constructed entirely of reinforced plate glass. The glass, through which the hotel guests could admire the view, shuddered and flexed alarmingly in the wind gusts. But it enabled Roger and Barbara to watch Cath check in, get her key and move off in the direction of her room.

They waited a few minutes before going to the front desk themselves. The room clerk looked at Roger in amazement.

"A view of t'parking lot?"

"Yes," said Roger emphatically, without giving a reason.

"I'm afraid of heights," Barbara said helpfully.

Room 29 was at the opposite end of the building from Cath and offered a fine view of the MG. The room had twin beds and avocado walls with a print of Marconi sending the world's first wireless message. The drinking glasses and the toilet seat were sealed in paper wrappers ("For your Protection").

"I knew it all along," chirped Barbara from the bathroom. "You *can* catch it from a glass or a toilet seat." There was no response from Roger. She poked her head into the bedroom. "Hello?"

Roger was leafing through the phonebook. "Be serious," he growled. "We have work to do."

"Sorry."

Roger set up a watch system to monitor the MG. Three on and three off. The watch would sit at the window and watch. The off-watch could sleep, bathe, read or eat. Barbara stood the one–four, Roger the four–seven and Barbara the seven–ten. Cath did not appear.

Roger took over at ten. He sat by the dark window. Barbara ran her second bath of the day. It was something to do.

"How long are we going to keep this up?" she yawned from the warmth of the steamy tub.

"Until she makes a move," he said. "And, Barbara, for God sakes turn off that stupid light or close the goddam bathroom door. I can't see!"

She waited a moment. "Roger?"

"What?"

"Take it easy." She reached out of the tub and quietly closed the door.

Cath took her time dressing. The outfit she had selected was the one Con had brought her from Scotland in 1964, the year after Derd was born. It was actually a kilt. The short skirt, in the Macleod plaid (her grandmother was a Macleod), was a pleated wrap-around held together at the bottom by a silver pin. It was worn with knee socks of the same plaid. The shoes were patent leather with silver buckles. The blouse was a ruffled piper's blouse with a lace jabot and the jacket black velvet with silver buttons.

The twelve-year-old jacket didn't fit and the skirt, wrapped as it was around a waist now many sizes too large, came to mid-thigh. The bizarre effect was one of a stout, putty-kneed, middle-aged woman playing dress-up in her daughter's clothes. Cath took no notice. This was Con's favorite. It had spent most of its life in the cedar chest and was good as new. She stood in front of the mirror and carefully applied the dark red lipstick she'd always worn, tracing the rouge slightly above the lip for fullness. She brushed the brittle, white hair, then coaxing the short perm into some semblance of the pageboy she used to wear. On top of this, finally, she placed the plaid tam-o-shanter, fitting it carefully to the side, at an angle, the way Con liked it.

She gazed into the mirror and smiled. The years fell away. She looked at her watch: 10:48. She picked up her purse and made sure she had her car keys and the key to her room. Satisfied, she sat on the edge of the bed, carefully spreading out the skirt in back so as not to wrinkle it. She took the pistol from the purse. For forty-two minutes she sat quietly, gun in hand, getting used to the feel of it. She scarcely moved except, from time to time, to stroke the black velvet sleeve above the wrist of the hand that held the weapon. At exactly 11:30, she got up, replaced the gun, turned out the light and left the room.

— * —

Barbara dreamt that all her relatives, living and dead, had chartered a bus from her home town in Wisconsin to Sandwich to
meet Roger. But Roger was shaking her. "Let's go!" She suffered
the tiny terror of switching realities.

"Grandma's alive again," she murmured.

"Barbara, wake up! Cath's getting into her car."

They went out the side door. Cath had flooded the MG. Blue
smoke mixed with the wind gusts and cracked the whip around
the parking lot.

They followed Cath out the Waterford Bridge Road for several miles. There was almost no traffic. Finally, on the edge of
town, she turned up a dark, narrow street flanked, on one side,
by warehouses and, on the other, by factory tenements. An abandoned railroad track with grass growing between the ties paral-
leled the road on the warehouse side. The track dead-ended in a
mound of earth. Fifty yards further, the street turned sharp right.
In the angle of the turn, next to a warehouse, was a bright blue
octagonal building. It looked like an old speakeasy and had
orange portholes instead of windows. Outside, over the street, a
neon sign blinked

THE

DRUID

CIRCLE

Half a dozen cars were parked in front. Cath pulled the MG over
to the curb before the turn in the road. Roger passed her, went
around the corner and parked the Vega in front of a warehouse.
They could hear an amplified accordion and bass accompanying
a male trio. The Druid Circle was a nightclub.

They locked the car and walked back in time to see Cath disappear into the building. The neon sign blinked on and off several times, then blinked off and stayed off. Roger glanced at his
watch. It was 12:02. Closing time. As they approached the
entrance, the trio ended its set. The lights inside came on. They
paused at the entrance to study the glossy publicity photos in a

147

glass frame beneath the sparkledust title. "Appearing Nitely" it said. The smiling trio were "The Boyle Brothers." There was a scantily clad "exotic dancer" named Gayle Warning. And the fortune teller was Fedelm. "Fedelm Foretells the Future," it said. The picture of her was an old, tinted, Bruno of Hollywood photo, wet-lipped and provocative.

They went inside. A few middle-aged couples, reluctant to leave, fingered nearly empty beer glasses. A fisherman had passed out at the bar.

"Sorry, sor," said a heavy-set man in shirtsleeves. "Closin' up."

"We're friends of Fedelm," Roger said.

"Jus' through the kitchen, then. She's in her dressin' room. Dere's a lady wit' her."

Cath walked through the sour-smelling pantry into the dark corridor. She stopped before an unpainted plywood door. It bore a red Dyno-mite plastic label: "Fedelm." Under the label was a sparkledust gold star with part of a point missing. Cath reached into her purse and withdrew the tiny handgun. She flicked off the safety and stared at the door. She imagined her adversary: tall, slim, strong, shoulders as broad as Con's but tapering to a waist no larger than two hands' breadth; the famous red hair to her buttocks; the famous saber legs with colt ankles and highly arched feet "like crescent moons." Was it Con said that or Des or the newspapers? Cath hesitated and leaned against the wall. She was losing her nerve. She almost put the gun back in her purse. But when she heard the man's voice behind the door, her fury surged. Her face contorted and she threw her full weight against the door. It burst from its feeble hinges with a splintering crash and fell into the dressing room. The mammoth woman sitting before the mirror screamed.

Cath stared in horror at the hennaed hippo before her. The monster weighed at least three hundred pounds. She completely hid the chair she sat on. The little man with her was an ancient, emaciated Chinese. He wore a soiled apron, no shirt, a cook's cap and smoked a pipe. He was about to pour whiskey into two paper cups. The fat woman had smeared lipstick on the top half of her astonished open mouth. The bottom half disappeared in massive folds of flesh and multiple chins. Rhinestone earrings sparkled beneath the dyed red afro frizz and rhinestone bracelets pressed the bloat around piling-sized wrists. The costume was grotesque: an enormous green-and-glittergold double-knit slack-suit. One pantleg was hiked up, showing an Ace bandage wrapped about a phlebitic ankle, thick as a tree. On her swollen feet she wore gold space shoes. She looked like a new truck.

The woman screamed again. Cath gasped and dropped the gun. It struck the floor and went off with a sharp crack. The bullet hit a leg of the chair, shattering it. The chair collapsed and the great bulk slowly rolled over onto the floor, screaming continuously. Cath turned and ran into Roger and Barbara. They hurried her through a side door. She collapsed on the sidewalk outside. Barbara thought she would melt into the pavement, leaving only her clothing, like the wicked witch. Cath moaned and tried to weep. Her bête noir, obese and clawless, was gone.

# CHAPTER 21

"Thursday, 22 July," Barbara wrote. "A miracle we weren't caught. Minutes elapsed before we made getaway. Cath carried to Vega. I drove. Roger flooded MG. Something about fuel pump. Returned to hotel same way we came. Absolutely certain RCMP patrol car will flash by any second. Pinned to curb, manacled, arraigned, found guilty of aiding and abetting dangerous armed psychotic, exiled forever to Sable Island. Phew! But nothing happened. Nothing appeared in paper this morning or evening. Concluded Druid Circle must wish low profile for some reason: expired liquor license, friendly card game in back room, brothel upstairs. Whatever. Nothing happened. And no one was hurt. Except Cath. She can't speak. Or won't."

They decided Cath would have to be flown home. As she couldn't travel alone, Roger's sister Jane was called. Jane agreed to help and would arrive in St. John's next afternoon. Roger then called a warehouse company that specialized in automobiles. They'd send a man to pick up the MG for winter storage.

That evening, Barbara phoned Spencer. Derdriu answered the phone on the first ring. "Hallo?" she said, her voice full of expectation. But when she heard who it was she became sullen.

"Oh. It's you."

"Hi," Barbara said. "How was your visit with Uncle Des?"

Derdriu ignored the question. "Have you found my father, yet?" Her voice trembled.

"Derd . . ."

"Or are you waitin' on the body to check the dental records?"

Barbara took a breath. "Please let me speak to Spencer, Derdriu."

"Can't you leave him in peace, for God's sake?" the child sobbed, and hung up.

An hour later Barbara called again and got Spencer. "She's sweet to the old man," he said, "but impudent as hell to the rest of us. Christ, in my day she'd've had her mouth washed out with soap by now."

"Best go easy," Barbara said. "Spence . . ." She chose her words carefully. "When Con was reported missing a month ago, Derdriu didn't respond. At all. She seemed . . . disinterested. But now, with Roger and me in Newfoundland, she's reacted for the first time. She acts threatened; like a child with a secret about to be divulged. I think she knows he's alive. I think she's known it all along. And, for reasons of her own, she's trying to keep us away from him."

"Well, Christ, if he stays lost he's worth a million bucks."

"Oh, Spence, come on. She doesn't care about the insurance money. She's only twelve."

"How old was Cleopatra?"

Without going into detail, Barbara told him what had happened to Cath and that Jane would bring her home. She gave him the arrival time of their connecting flight to Bradley International. "By the way," she added, "we're staying at the Signal Hill Hotel if you need to reach us."

"Hell," he grunted, "I mailed some stuff up to you care of Angus the other day. Mostly yard stuff. But there was a letter for Cath that I opened. It didn't make much sense to me so I sent it along." He paused. "You bastards still in love?"

Barbara sighed. "Ask me again when this is over."

Roger woke Friday morning and realized what it was that had been nagging him for forty-eight hours. There was something wrong with Angus's story of the inflatable. If the dinghy had been destroyed by a ship's propellers, how had the engine escaped damage? He drew diagrams of a hypothetical collision, from several angles. The answer would not reveal itself. Finally he phoned Angus at Job's wharf.

"Was the engine damaged at all?"

"Oiy can't say, Roger."

"What about the cuts? Were they athwartships or fore and aft?"

"Oiy can't say. But Tom Dolan's boy Mick'll take you to Puffin Cove if you loik. Dere's no road in, Roger. Ye'll have to go by skiff."

It was arranged that Roger and Barbara would be lunch guests at noon aboard *Stornoway* after which Angus would drive Roger to Dolan's wharf at Portugal Cove. Barbara could have the afternoon off.

Barbara wore a dress and Roger his only jacket. Angus welcomed them aboard the dragger. The vessel was steel, eighty feet overall and painted bright yellow with a black-and-white checkerboard cover stripe. Angus's crew of three, Borden, Almon and Burnell, the cook, stood at a respectable distance, smiling shyly. They were all spruced up, caps off, hair combed and each holding an enameled cup. There was a sense of occasion. Roger and Barbara were handed enameled cups.

"Cocktoils," said Angus.

The drink was an evil concoction of dark rum and hot water called screech. It made Barbara want to. She nursed hers until Burnell served lunch. He loaded a plate especially for her. After three screeches, he had fallen in love.

"Fish an' brewis," he murmured confidentially, "an' cods' tongues."

"Wonderful," she said.

She couldn't get the fish and brewis past her nose. F & B is an old Grand Banks staple: salt cod and sea biscuit softened and mashed in boiling water and served awash in sow-belly fat. The fried cods' tongues, considered a delicacy, took a little getting used to. Barbara smiled at Burnell, praised his cuisine and pretended to eat. He was so pleased he had another screech.

"My ass for a BLT," she wrote later. "Roger, of course, ate everything. By the end of lunch he even acquired a slight Newfie accent and was invited to join the crew of *Stornoway* permanently."

After lunch Barbara thanked Angus, kissed Burnell on the cheek and left. An hour and several screeches later, Angus and Roger stumbled ashore, got into Angus's old Dodge pickup and weaved out of St. John's on the Portugal Cove Road. Barbara drove back to the hotel and checked with the practical nurse Roger had hired to care for Cath. "I'd be grateful if you'd stay until Mrs. Pond arrives," she said. "It shouldn't be much after six unless the plane is late."

The book stall in the lobby had nothing to offer so Barbara returned to room 29, washed her hair and settled down with Cliff's dog-eared copy of *The Criminal Use of False Identification*. To her surprise, it was fascinating.

Cliff had marked a section entitled "I.D.I.—Infant Death Identity." The section outlined a method by which anyone can assume a new identity. The imposter searches through the obituaries of old newspapers for the death notice of an infant or child who, if he were still alive, would be approximately the age of the imposter. With nothing more than the infant's name, place of birth and the names of his parents, the imposter may apply for a copy of the infant's birth certificate. This is possible because birth and death records are seldom correlated. The imposter now assumes the infant's identity and, with his birth certificate, applies for passport, driver's license, credit cards, et cetera.

Barbara leafed through the entire pamphlet. But she kept coming back to the IDI section. She read it several times. Finally she tossed the pamphlet on the bed and looked at her watch: 2:10. Her hair was dry and she was free until almost six.

As the old Dodge chugged to the top of the hill above Portugal Cove, the rain started to fall. Roger had a headache. And when he got out of the truck at Dolan's Wharf, his legs seemed paralyzed.

"Pay no attention, Roger," said Angus. "'Tis but a temporary dysfunction of the blood brought on by yer system's cryin' need for supplementary screech. Ah. Dere's Mick."

Mick Dolan, "Tom's boy," was about sixty. Like most Newfie fishermen who subsist on potatoes, biscuit and whatever they catch, Mick paid scant attention to vitamins and such. He had two teeth left, one top left and one bottom right. He nodded enthusiastically at Roger, produced a gaping, bi-tusked grin and nearly shook his hand off.

"Foin day," he said, squinting at the drizzle. They walked to the end of the wharf where a shack teetered on thin pilings. Roger was relieved to hear that Mick had brought the inflatable down from Puffin Cove for the value of the rubber. There would be no need now for a thirty-mile trip in an open boat in the rain with a hangover.

The shack smelled of fish and salt. Through an open trap in the floor, Roger could see the shallow water fifteen feet below. The mud bottom was covered with fish heads and guts. In the shack, on a work table, parts of the Seagull soaked in gasoline. The gas tank and lower unit, undamaged, leaned against a wall.

"She's been in t'water," Mick said sensibly. "But Oi'll get she runnin', never fear. And build she a proper skiff too."

The inflatable had been rolled up and flung in a corner. Mick brought it to the work table and unrolled it. Roger saw immediately that the dinghy was in far better condition than he'd been led to expect. At least two compartments were probably still airtight though deflated. It was clear that Mick, who had a poor opinion of rubber boats, didn't think much of this one and had probably assumed she was more seriously damaged simply because she was limp and deflated when he found her.

There were some cuts, most of them athwartships. However, one cut, the longest, was fore and aft. It ran the whole length of the starboard forward compartment, from the oarlock to the painter ring.

"Lord Jaysus," said Angus, running his hand along the sliced compartment. "T'is wunnerful perpuller can make a cut like that!"

Roger agreed. The cut was too straight and too clean. So were the others. A propeller blade is angled for pitch and makes a series of short, shredding cuts, not a single clean cut. "It looks," said Roger, "as if she was scuttled with a rigging knife."

"Room M1, on the mezzanine," said the lady at the information desk.

Barbara walked across the marble lobby of the Hall of Records and up a cherub-and-grapes mahogany staircase that would not have been out of place on the old *Mauretania*. However, splendor and pretense stopped at the bleak frontier of the mezzanine. Room M1 was at the end of a fluorescent-lit, green plywood hallway with a brown linoleum floor. It all smelled of Lestoil.

The supervisor of room M1, "Certificates, Death," was a serious young East Indian woman in a sari. She led Barbara down a corridor of filing cabinets. They arrived at K–L. The supervisor was apologetic.

"Someday all this will be on tape. But, for the moment"—she pulled open drawer KA–KH—"it's fiddle and squint." She nodded and left.

Barbara looked at the file drawer dividers. It was only a hunch. But her palms were sweating.

She thumbed through the dividers: "Katz, Kay, Kay, Kayle, Kaynor, Kean." There were lots of Keans: Kean A, B, C, and D: "Kean, Daggitt, Dalsey, Daniel, Daniel, Daniel, Darius, Daubie, David." Three Davids:

"Kean, David B., b. 3/3/91 Quidi Vidi Hbr, d. 12/1/72." Eighty-one years old when he died.

"Kean, David M., b. 7/5/57, Petty Hbr, d. 9/1/75." Barely nineteen. Too young.

"Kean, David R., b. 6/6/35 Topsail, d. 9/10/39." He would be forty-one; same age as Con.

Barbara followed the indexing and wrote down the heartbreaking facts. David R. Kean, age four, drowned at Pouch Cove with his fisherman father, Anthony, thirty-three. His mother, Maive, died of consumption three months later at the age of twenty-two. Barbara stared at her notes and wondered at God's priorities.

She thanked the supervisor, walked down the mahogany staircase and across the lobby to Room 7. There, she filled out form BN 2773, "Birth Certificate, Photocopy, Application for," and handed it to the gay middle-aged male clerk wearing the necklace. The clerk sighed and peered at her over half glasses.

"Dear," he said wearily, "are you David R. Kean?"

"No, sir," she said.

"That's a relief," he murmured. He studied the form. "May I ask your relationship to the applicant?"

"Umm . . . he's my employer."

"I see. Well tell your employer he'll have to apply in person." He looked at the application again and frowned. "Kean . . . Kean. One moment, please." He got up and disappeared through a doorway.

Barbara felt a strong urge to run. Maybe the birth and death records were correlated in Canada. Maybe IDI was old stuff to them. How many years could you get on Sable Island for impersonating a drowned child? She felt sneaky and cynical and was about to take a step toward the door when the clerk returned.

"Just as I thought," he said with a trace of smugness. "I have a 2773 showing we issued your Mr. Kean a photocopy of his birth certificate on fifteen March. That's only four months ago." He peered at her over his glasses again. "What does he do with them? Paper the walls?"

Barbara thanked him and left. Her pulse hammered in her neck as she recrossed the marble lobby. It couldn't be a coincidence! It couldn't! While *Hound of Ulster* lay on Joe Yedresek's mooring from the tenth to the seventeenth of March, Con had come to St. John's to arrange for his new identity.

She stopped and leaned against a pillar to catch her breath. After a moment, she left the building by the side entrance which opened on the parking lot. A light rain had begun to fall. She heard a car door slam nearby.

"Mrs. Foster?"

He was young. No more than twenty-one. He wore a ponytail and one ear was pierced. He opened the rear door of the Cadillac that blocked her Vega.

"Get in, please," he said.

Barbara froze. She saw the man in the back of the Fleetwood lean forward. "Get in, Mrs. Foster," he said. It was Marshall Leonetti.

# CHAPTER 22

Angus dropped Roger halfway up Signal Hill. The old Dodge pickup, needing a new radiator hose, refused to go farther.

Roger climbed the hill on foot. When he reached the hotel parking lot he noticed the Vega wasn't there. Irritated, he glanced at his watch: 5:05. Barbara still out and Jane's flight due in twenty minutes. Maybe Barbara had driven to the airport. He checked at the front desk to see if she had left word.

"Nor, sor," the desk clerk said. "No messages. But there's this." He handed Roger an envelope. "A fisherman brought it up from Job's wharf." The envelope bore the Truly's Boatyard logo. It was from Spencer and had been sent to Roger care of Angus.

"Thanks," Roger said. He started to open it.

"And, sir," the room clerk added, "there's a gentleman waiting for you in t'coffee shop." Roger had almost forgotten.

The man from the storage warehouse was supposed to come for Cath's MG. He slipped the envelope into the inside pocket of his jacket and hurried down the stairs to the coffee shop. On the bottom step he paused. At a table, with an empty coffee cup in front of him, sat Desmond Macroth.

Des rose politely as Roger came over. It was past cocktail time and the sight of Des, cold sober in a coffee shop in St. John's, was somehow menacing. However, the little dandy, hounds-toothed and bow-tied, smiled warmly. They shook hands.

"I'm sorry to barge in like this without calling," Des said.

"No problem," Roger answered. "But I hope this is a social visit that can wait because I'm in a hell of a hurry. Got to be at the airport in fifteen minutes."

"Perfect," Des said. "I'm due there too. I'll drive you." He smiled again. The blue eyes crinkled at the corners. "Because, Roger, I'm afraid this isn't a social visit that can wait."

Des had rented a Pinto. It was gold and had a crunched right front fender. The head lamp hung from its socket by wire ganglia like an outraged eye. Des drove slowly and smoked. He didn't speak until they reached the detour at the bottom of Signal Hill.

"I have heard," he said finally, "that you think my brother may be alive." Roger's scalp tingled and he felt dizzy for an instant. The burst headlight clanked against the grill. Roger looked out the window at the hard-hatted construction workers along the detour. They made him long for the simple life.

Des continued. "If I thought I could make a deal with you, Roger, I would." He paused. "I've been authorized to." Des stopped for a red light and carefully watched Roger for a response. There was none. "I thought not," he chuckled. The light changed and he swung the Pinto onto the airport road. "You don't disappoint me, Truly. You're as reliable and predictable as high tide."

Roger ignored the remark. He turned to Des.

"Was Con supposed to sink the boat?"

"Oh, my yes. And if he had, you and I would still be friends and not puttering about on this dark tundra."

"So it was planned? Right from the beginning?"

"No, Roger. Not from the beginning." Des lit another cigarette and inhaled deeply. "In the beginning, Con commissioned Rushton to design *Hound* for only one reason: he wanted to win the Jester Class of the transatlantic race. Nothing tricky, nothing mysterious. You know Con. He doesn't think business is proper work for a man of spirit. He thinks a man needs to do something extraordinary from time to time, to nourish his self-esteem, to give his life size and grandeur. Typical Celt. He wanted to win the *Ostar*, Roger. That's all there was to it. In the beginning.

"But circumstances changed. The sponsorship he had counted on was not forthcoming, money became tight and, very quickly, the boat became the rallying point and battleground of Con's twenty years' war with Cath."

Roger felt he was going to be told more than he needed to hear.

"Let's skip the details. What do you want from me?"

Des sighed patiently. "Ah, Roger, never ask an Irishman to skip details. To do so impoverishes the narrative and leaves the listener disappointed and underfed." He paused for another drag on his cigarette. "I want to convince you, Roger, that Con did what he did because it was his last chance for redemption. When I've convinced you, if I convince you, you'll know what I want."

Something in Des's voice at that moment . . . a tone both subdued and assured . . . commanded Roger's respect.

"You must understand," Des went on, "that since his marriage, Con has been in Cath's neurotic custody. He's been virtually under emotional house arrest. She has systematically sought to destroy everything that could conceivably divert his interest and attention from her. Everything. People, things, art. When she learned of his intention to enter the *Ostar* . . . long before the boat was built . . . her reaction was swift and retaliatory. She ordered a ten-thousand-dollar sable coat and charged it to the company. When the coat was sent back she fell ill imme-

160

diately and was admitted to hospital for a fortnight's observation at two hundred dollars a day. They treated her with lithium chloride. It did nothing. You can treat a manic depressive with medicine. But what medicine can you give a dues-paying, card-carrying cunt?

"Their final, catastrophic fight occurred one night in early February. Your boatyard had all but completed the yacht and Con's qualification trial was only a month away. Cath launched her final attack to dissuade him . . . to frighten him . . . blackmail him into abandoning the race. She lied that Derdriu was being persecuted at school because her father owed everybody in town. She lied that the first Selectman had said he should sell the boat and the house to pay his bills. She was in a frenzy that night. I was there, Roger, in the living room, standing between the two of them. Con was trembling with anger. He turned to her, finally, and said quietly, 'Very well then. I'll do as you ask. I'll sell the boat and abandon the race. If you divorce me.' Well, at that she grabbed a letter opener and turned on him. She screamed 'Muc!' That's Scots gaelic for 'pig.' 'Muc!' she screamed, and slashed at him. 'Never! . . . Never! . . . Muc! . . . Muc!' Derdriu ran downstairs in her pajamas and rushed to her father. It took the three of us to subdue Cath."

Des butted his cigarette in the ashtray, reached for another and changed his mind. He sighed. "She was readmitted to hospital for observation. Of course she fooled the therapists, as usual, and was released. They could never agree on what was wrong with her, if anything. Con had asked her for a divorce a dozen times with the same result." Des drove in silence for a moment. "That night," he said quietly, "was the end. That night, Con's purpose in entering the *Ostar* changed."

Roger pondered the mystery of marriage. How could Con have allowed himself . . . ? But he stopped in mid-pontification, remembering his own marriage to Katya which had failed for reasons probably no less preposterous.

"At the end of February," Des continued, "Con came to me with a plan that absolutely terrified me. At first. But I thought it through, and, after a bit, saw it was his only salvation. The plan he proposed would leave Cath financially secure but enable him to disappear without a trace to pursue the career for which he was naturally born."

"And what career is that?" Roger asked suddenly.

Des hesitated. "I think if I told you, Roger, you might make a wrong value judgment. I don't know how you rate vocational merit. Which do you place higher on the work value scale? Doctors, or Wimbledon finalists? The president of General Motors, or the concertmaster of the Vienna Philharmonic?" He hesitated again. "I can tell you this, Roger. Con's work is neither trivial nor insignificant. It is work for which he has prodigious talent. And work which, I think, will make the world a better place."

They reached the airport. Des looked around for a parking place and found one near the General Aviation area. He shut off the Pinto and turned to Roger.

"Derdriu knows," he said. "She's intensely proud of what he's done and, when she's eighteen, plans to join him. By the way, it upset her very much that you and Barbara came up here looking for Con. She loves you both. But she loves her father more." The blue eyes were melancholy. "I love him too, Roger. He's a good and talented man and I want him to have this chance."

Roger watched an Argus aircraft lumber into the sky behind the administration building. "What you're asking then, I take it, is for me to go away and forget all about Con Macroth."

"Yes."

Roger followed the plane for a moment. "Des," he said quietly, "your earnest and noble entreaty on behalf of your brother might have moved me deeply. Except that I happen to know you're one of the three beneficiaries of his life insurance."

"Roger . . ."

"If I go away and forget about Con, you get five hundred thousand dollars. That simple fact kicks the shit out of your petition."

"The money is yours, Roger," Des said without hesitation. "I'll sign it over to you right here. Right now."

Roger smiled. A half a million! That'd pay off the yard mortgage, replank the schooner and then some. The Argus flew into the sun and out of sight. "No," he said. He turned and faced Des.

"Do you have any idea how many thousands of dollars and how many hours of vigilance your 'good and talented man' cost the Canadian Rescue Coordinating Center, the CCG and the U.S. Coasties? Do you know how much trouble he caused Lieutenant Quinn at SAR in New York, Captain Castaign and the crew of *Bearn*, Foliot, Mademoiselle deLille . . ."

"Ah, the inaccessible Mademoiselle deLille!" Des remembered.

"And Captain Jacobsen and the crew of *Oslofjord?* What about the hours of devotion and overtime put in by the guys at my yard? Are you aware that my father trusted your good and talented brother and was nearly wiped out for his pains?" Roger shook his head. "No," he said. "I don't see that Con deserves a chance. Not this way. You don't break the law to solve domestic problems or to seize missed opportunities. So don't expect a compassionate judgment from me. A criminal act has been committed. I can't be sentimental about fraud. And cheating his insurance companies out of a million and a half dollars is hard-nosed, gimlet-eyed fraud. I'm very goddam sorry!"

Des gazed at Roger and sighed. "I had no idea you were sentimental about insurance companies. Well. I'm sorry too, Roger."

Des's eyes shifted then. Roger turned and followed his gaze. Fifty yards away, beside a silver-and-red twin-engined airplane, stood Marshall and Arch Leonetti with Barbara between them. Roger jerked his head back to face Des. The dapper little man was smiling apologetically down the barrel of a Smith and Wesson .38 revolver.

# CHAPTER 23

$\mathcal{J}$ane Pond couldn't believe her eyes. Her flight had landed on schedule. As the DC-8 taxied toward the Air Canada gate, passing a Coast Guard hanger and a group of private planes tied down in the General Aviation section, Jane looked out her window and saw Barbara and Roger standing with Marshall Leonetti and Des. Her first instinct was to wave. "Yoo-hoo," she said, without thinking, and waved. Then she became disoriented. St. John's, Newfoundland, was the end of the earth. What in the world were Desmond Macroth and Marshall Leonetti doing in St. John's with Barbara and her brother?

As the DC-8 moved on, Jane leaned forward in her seat as far as she could to keep them in view. Before she lost sight of them she saw Roger and Barbara climb into a silver-and-red airplane whose propellers were already turning.

An Air Canada representative met her inside the passenger gate.

"Mrs. Pond?"

"Yes."

"Welcome to St. John's."

"Thank you."

"I have the tickets and seat reservations for you and Mrs. Macroth on Air Canada's Flight 691 departing six-fifty. Your brother and Mrs. Foster have been detained and won't be able to meet you. However, an ambulance is bringing Mrs. Macroth from the Signal Hill Hotel. We'll have a wheelchair waiting in the handicapped persons area at six."

"Today?"

"Why yes." He looked at his watch. "In an hour."

"Thank you," she said again and took the tickets. The attendant tipped his hat and left.

Jane felt a swirl of fear. Roger and Barbara "detained"? Is that what they called being in an airplane with Marshall Leonetti? Why was her flight home with Cath, scheduled for tomorrow, changed to today? Ambulance? Wheelchair? Not a bit like Roger. Or Barbara. She walked past the baggage claim to a bank of public telephones and made a credit-card call to her father in Sandwich. There was no answer. Her fear turned to determination. She did not like or trust Marshall Leonetti. She hung up the phone and stepped out on the observation deck. The silver-and-red airplane was at the far end of the field warming up. Perhaps if she looked at it hard enough, it would develop engine trouble and stop. But the twin had already begun its take-off roll. As the airplane streaked down the field, rotated and rose easily into the air, Jane made out the registration on the side. N1742F. She wrote the numbers on the back of her hand with a lipstick. Then she went to the phone and placed another call.

Chaim Gold was preparing Chinese quail eggs when his phone rang. He moved the steamer off the burner and picked up the wall receiver.

"Good evening," he said. "And now the Jewish weather: Clear

165

tonight but look for high, scattered tsuris before morning." He listened for a moment. "Do you know what kind of airplane it was? Cessna? Beechcraft? No. Doesn't matter. Yes, I can. Good work, Jane. Make your flight home as arranged. I'll call Spence later. Phone me when you get in."

He hung up, turned off the stove and called a man he played squash with once a week. The man gave him the phone number of the General Aviation office of the FAA in Westfield, Massachusetts. N1742F was a Piper Chieftain owned by Mumford Airways and leased to the Macroth Corporation of New London. The airplane was based at Trumbull Airport, Groton, and had filed a flight plan two days earlier from Groton to Halifax via Bar Harbor.

"How come St. John's wasn't in their flight plan?" Chaim asked.

"What an airplane does in Canada is Canada's business," the supervisor said. "We have no jurisdiction there. However, they're always very cooperative. I suggest you call traffic control in St. John's and request details from them."

Roger sat in the right front seat of the Chieftain and watched the altimeter needle stop at 6,500 feet. In the pilot's seat to Roger's left, Arch Leonetti spoke to Sydney, Nova Scotia, by radio. After a moment, he removed his headset, cranked in the new course and put the airplane on auto. Barbara, in the seat behind Roger, stared silently out the window. Marshall Leonetti, across the aisle from Barbara, worked on a *New York Times* crossword puzzle. The rest of the airplane was empty. Des had stayed in St. John's to wait for a commercial flight.

Roger had never had a gun pointed at him before; except once, in a dinghy race, when he was early at the committee-boat end of the line and the starting cannon nearly blew his Interclub out of the water. Having a revolver—a loaded revolver—pointed at his chest was an exotic experience for Roger. His initial response, typically Wasp, was well-mannered disbelief. "My God, Des!" he'd said, as if Des had sipped the water from his fingerbowl. But disbelief had quickly given way to chilling apprehension. "I thought," Des had said, "I could persuade you by appealing to your sensibilities. I failed. Now it's up to Marshall Leonetti."

On the plane, Leonetti had been brief and specific. "Truly's Boatyard," he said, "is in violation of EPA regulations regarding tidal wetlands. For you to comply with agency guidelines would mean a loss of yard working area of more than sixty percent. In a word, you would be out of business. However, don't feel too bad. The place is a firetrap. Three of your four sheds are wood and the electrical wiring is a disgrace. I'd hate to think what would happen to the town of Sandwich and all its beautiful eighteenth-century houses if a fire got started at your place some windy night."

That was that. The adventure was over. Roger never claimed to be a hero. There would be no last-minute reprieve. The bad guys had won. Leonetti, skillful and deadly, had gotten what he'd come for without fuss or bother. Or a gun. Des had needed the gun. Not Leonetti.

It took Chaim nearly an hour to get a clear line to St. John's air-traffic control. He finally got through to a very British, ex-RAF type who had the aroma of pipe tobacco in his voice. The handlebar mustache nearly tickled Chaim's nose through the phone.

"Pruitt, here," the airy voice said. "Your aircraft filed VFR for Halifax, ETA 2130 hours which is, I think, a bit optimistic for a Chieftain with a thirty-knot headwind. You say you are related to one of the passengers?"

"Yes," Chaim lied.

To Mr. . . . ah . . . Leonetti, then?"

"No. To Roger Truly."

"Truly. Truly." Chaim could hear papers being shuffled. "Hm. That's odd. We request all general-aviation aircraft intending to leave Canada to file an Inspection Report for Customs and related matters. The form is quite similar to the U.S., actually: should include, among other things, the names of all passengers. The only passenger listed here is 'Leonetti, M.' You're quite sure there were two other passengers?"

"At least two," Chaim said. "Roger Truly and his fiancée, Barbara Foster. I'm certain they are aboard and equally certain they are aboard against their wishes."

Pruitt paused. "Are you suggesting," he said after a moment, "that people are being kidnapped aboard one-seven-four-two-Foxtrot?"

"Yes."

"Might there be firearms aboard?"

"Possibly."

"You're not certain?"

"No."

"Are you a policeman?"

"No."

"May I have your name, please?"

Chaim gave Pruitt his name, address and occupation (senior surface analyst, U.S. Weather Bureau, National Oceanographic and Atmospheric Administration, Rockefeller Center, New York, New York). Pruitt seemed impressed. At least he wrote it all down. "Truly and I are cousins," Chaim added.

There was a short silence while Pruitt completed his notes. "Very well," he said finally. "You will understand, Mr. Gold, that I cannot very well order out the entire Royal Canadian Air Force simply because of allegations made by you over the telephone. However, there is the technicality of the Aircraft Inspection Report filed by four-two-Fox. While the AIR is voluntary for all pilots, failure to provide the information requested can result in a delay of the aircraft for Customs inspection. I'll get on to C&I, Halifax, and précis the problem for them."

"What might that do?"

"Well, I can't give you a guarantee, can I? But C&I could delay the aircraft for six hours or more; especially if what you say is true; or if they find something improper aboard."

Chaim wanted a guarantee. "Which reminds me," he said. "The pilot is a very heavy smoker. Very heavy. Tell them to look for hash on the airplane." It was just a guess.

—— ✳ ——

The Chieftain stayed locked on 238 degrees. Arch studied the Halifax sectional chart. Marshall Leonetti looked up from his crossword puzzle.

"Anybody got a pen? Mine's dry."

Roger reached inside his jacket and passed back a ballpoint. During this, his hand brushed against the still-unopened envelope from Spencer which had been mailed c/o Angus. He took it out and opened it.

There was a receipted bill for twenty gallons of Interlux, an inquiry on the cost of sister-framing and refastening a Concordia, a workmen's comp form for one of the haulers and a letter to Mrs. Con Macroth. Spencer had opened it and scrawled "Is this important?" in the margin. The letter was painstakingly typed on stationery bearing the letterhead of the "Sunset House, a Full Nursing-Care Facility, Dartmouth, Nova Scotia." At first, Roger thought it might be one of the nursing homes Cath had been in or was applying to. Then he read the letter. It was dated July 16.

> Dear Madame:
>
> I pray you will excuse this intrusion at your time of grief. I wait what I hope is an appropriate interval before writing.
>
> Please. Can you tell me if your husband recently reported missing in the sea is the same Con Macroth who was my brilliant student at Dalhousie University, Halifax, from 1952 to 1955? We lose touch over the years which is a great pity for me. He was like a son. I do not know he cares for the sea. I was confident he will make a magnificent career in music. A most extraordinary artist!
>
> I have now failing eyesight and the nurse must write this letter. Be sure, Madame, of my gratitude for any response and compassion in your grievous loss.
>
> Most cordially,
> (Dr.) Frederick B. Schneider

Roger read the letter twice. The phrase that jumped off the page at him was "magnificent career in music." Des had called it "career for which he was naturally born" and "work which was neither trivial nor insignificant."

So that was it. Music. Roger had trouble taking a career in music seriously. It was something he knew nothing about. And, while he could admire a theoretical physicist without knowing a thing about physics, he couldn't give a musician or music the same esteem. He knew it was a prejudice; probably inherited from his mother who, when she met a prominent cellist years ago at a party, said, "Yes, but what do you really do?"

Roger read the letter again. He was about to turn around in his seat to hand it to Barbara when he felt Arch Leonetti watching him. Arch had replaced his headset. "Buckle up," he said. They were twenty minutes out.

Arch spoke to Halifax Approach at Trafalgar, adjusted his altimeter and homed on the Fax VOR at Devon.

Fifteen minutes later, Approach turned him over to the tower. He was cleared to pattern altitude and to land on runway two-four. He confirmed, dropped his gear and half flaps and entered left base. Before he turned final the tower broke in.

"Correction, four-two Fox. Please abort. Turn right zero-niner-five, climb fifteen hundred and return Devon VOR. No traffic."

"Shit!" Arch said. He firewalled the throttles, retracted everything and put the Chieftain into a lot tighter turn than was needed.

Marshall Leonetti leaned forward. "What are you doing?"

"Going back to Dear Mom. There's probably a canuck gooneybird tryin' to roost."

The tower came back. "Ah, four-two Fox, you are now clear to land runway two-four. Altimeter three-zero-one-two, wind two-three-zero at one-zero. Sorry about the delay. Please exit taxiway seven and proceed area B for Bravo. Confirm."

Arch confirmed. Four minutes later they were on the ground and taxiing along the access to Area B next to the administration building. The Chieftain's landing lights picked up a jeep with "Follow Me" stenciled across the back.

"Pretty cool," said Arch and followed.

He was waved to park between a pair of DH Otters. He swung the Chieftain ninety degrees and shut down. Marshall Leonetti walked aft to open the cabin door.

"Mr. Truly and Mrs. Foster will please stay put," he said over his shoulder. "We'll only be here a few minutes." He opened the door and looked into the unsmiling faces of two uniformed Customs and Immigration officers. Behind them was an RCMP officer and, behind him, an RCMP van with its engine running and its Rotabeam flashing. Leonetti smiled. "Gentlemen," he said.

They nearly took the airplane apart. In going through Arch's toilet kit, they found not hashish but cocaine. Over an ounce of it was concealed in the bottom half of his jumbo tube of Ultra Brite. There were no firearms aboard. However, in the aircraft's diminutive galley, next to a can of Reddi Wip, they found a canister of Chemical Mace. The Chieftain was grounded indefinitely. Marshall and Arch were loaded into the RCMP van and taken away.

After being questioned and released, Roger and Barbara stared at each other, bewildered. Roger went to the bathroom. Barbara sat in the Customs and Immigration office. She was numb. The last clear picture she had of herself was in the St. John's Hall of Records. She remembered coming out the side door, trembling with excitement at the discovery she'd made. She couldn't wait to tell Roger. But then the terrible Leonettis were waiting and her terror began. The fear had driven everything out of her head. Now she was just numb. Now nothing mattered except to go home and forget all about Con Macroth.

The Customs man gave the passports back to Barbara. "By the way," he said, "Mr. Truly is to call his cousin in New York. Collect."

"Cousin?"

He handed her a memo with the phone number on it. "You can use the desk phone," he said.

Barbara looked at the memo and almost cheered with relief. The number was Chaim's apartment in Chelsea. She dialed.

"Chaim!" she cried. "Nobody ever saved by life before! I feel helpless and melodramatic!"

"Tut, my dear Foster. It is merely Gold's Eye-in-the-Sky Service. . . . Beaucoup watch-over-you whenever you roam-from-home, dum-de-dum. Where's yours Truly?"

"In the john. Oh, wait. He's out. Hold on." She yelled at Roger through the doorway. But he disappeared. "Whoa a minute, Chaim." She put down the phone and ran out of the office in time to see Roger enter a phone booth next to the Québecair counter. She went to the booth and pushed open the door. Roger was dialing. "Chaim's on the phone in the Customs office," she said.

Roger waved her away. "In a minute." He spoke into the phone. "Sunset House?" He closed the door in her face.

She blinked and stalked back to the office. "Sorry," she said. "He's busy." She sighed. "I don't know what's the matter with him. But I know what's the matter with me. I'm too old for this crap. I'm dying for peace and quiet in Connecticut. I can't wait for the fall foliage and woodsmoke and chrysanthemums."

"You sound pissed-off wistful," he said quietly.

She felt the beginnings of a tear in the corner of one eye. "Yeah. I guess. Don't be nice to me. I'm having a little weekend self-pity." She blew her nose. "Oh, Chaim, I was as excited as he was in the beginning. All this big brave stuff! It was challenging. I felt righteous and indignant. But it's changed him. He's become haunted by it. He's lost his sense of humor. All he has now is a sense of importance. He's turned into a regular U.S. Certified grade-A son of a bitch. And he's impatient and rude with me. He never was before. Not ever."

"Barbara." Chaim spoke softly. "In spite of his phlegmatic and rumpled image, Roger has always sought the Perilous Labor. He's never really been at peace with himself. I think you may bring it to him finally. But, in the meantime, Roger is very like the man he's hunting. And, Barbara, if you will permit me to quote the prophet Shapiro: Don't *hock* too much *a chainik;* you didn't have to come along."

Over after-dinner drinks at the Lord Halifax, Roger gave her a long, mellow look. He smiled. He seemed relaxed and happy.

172

Barbara too had begun to feel the return of her vital signs. The dinner had been marvelous. Her feet were no longer cold. Her blood seemed to be circulating again. And something like desire was beginning to nudge her lower parts pleasantly.

"Let's have an after-drink drink," he said.

While they waited for the cognac, she took his hand. Though the long voyage was over and they were going home tomorrow, she still wanted the satisfaction of telling him what she'd found in the Hall of Records.

"My God!" His eyes were shining by the time she finished. "You're magnificent," he said honestly. "Also gorgeous."

The cognac arrived. Roger leaned across the table. He swirled the brandy in his snifter for a moment and gazed at her. Barbara was virtually certain he was going to propose and name the date.

"What would you say," he murmured, "if I told you Con Macroth was a closet musician?"

Barbara was so unprepared for the question her mouth fell open. "Huh?"

He reached into his jacket and handed her the letter from Dr. Schneider. It took her a moment to tuck away her disappointment and reorient herself.

"It makes sense," she said after reading through it once. "I'm sure it's the same Con Macroth."

"But wasn't he . . . isn't he . . . just another after-dinner Cole Porter player? I mean, isn't music just a hobby to him?"

Barbara shrugged. "I guess not," she said, handing back the letter. "In fact, now that I think of it, Derdriu told me ages ago he had a practice keyboard he took with him on business trips. Unless he was serious it seems a little weird for an urban developer to take a practice keyboard with him on business trips. He also had a pedal board in the cellar, until Cath threw it out."

"What the hell's a pedal board?"

"Practice thing for the organ. Organists play the bass notes with their feet."

"Then he's an organist?"

"Roger, I don't know, dear. Anymore than you do. All I said was the letter makes sense." Suddenly she was tired.

"Well, we'll sort it all out in the morning when we visit Dr. Schneider."

"What?"

"When we visit Dr. Schneider at the Sunset House nursing home. Tomorrow. It's not far."

"Roger." She could feel the chords in her neck. "We're going home tomorrow. Flying home to forget all about Con Macroth. Remember Leonetti? The one who's going to burn down the yard?"

"He can't. He's in jail."

"Don't be naive! He'll be out by breakfast. We've got to go home and string barbed wire!"

"After we've talked to Dr. Schneider."

Barbara got up from the table. "Leonetti will burn down your boatyard!"

"He won't."

"He will."

"He will not!"

"He will so!"

"Fuck 'im!"

Barbara wanted to say "Fuck you!" as loud as she could. But there were two blue-haired Halifax ladies at the next table eavesdropping. She gave them each an icy smile and walked out.

They slept the fitful sleep of the exhausted, on opposite sides of the hotel bed, facing out. Between them there was enough napping room for a full-grown lion. They had become transient strangers.

Barbara had a nightmare. She dreamed she was going to marry Angus's seacook, Burnell. Betsy gave her a bridal shower and the entire sixth grade was there, eating cods' tongues and drinking orange ice and screech punch. Barbara woke in a sweat. A church bell rang five times. She got up, ran a bath almost to the top of the tub and got in. The luxury of hot water, she thought, the beneficent and curative powers of very hot water were deep and miraculous. "My very own Lourdes," she said as the crippling tension of the past few days evaporated into the blessed water.

174

Last night, she'd made up her mind to catch the early flight home, with or without Roger. Now, floating in steamy equanimity, she reconsidered. There was, after all, a midmorning flight. If Roger would promise to catch the midmorning flight after seeing this Dr. What's-his-name, she'd go with him to the nursing home.

"Okay," Roger said at breakfast. "I promise."

They arrived at Sunset House a little before nine A.M. The cab dropped them under the porte cochère of a formidable Victorian pile of limestone and wrought-iron gingerbread. The house stood among copper beeches and chestnut trees on the top of a hill above Dartmouth. Narrow gauge cement walks crisscrossed the acres of lawn that fell away from the mansion. They served as avenues for a dozen wicker wheelchairs occupied by very old people and propelled by nurses and attendants.

Next to a yew tree at the bottom of the lawn, away from the cement walks and the other patients, sat an old man alone. His wispy, white baby hair moved gently in the soft breeze. It was a warm, sunny morning. Nevertheless he was wrapped in a heavy shawl.

The nurse, robust and apple-cheeked and carrying two folding chairs, marched down the lawn several paces ahead of Roger and Barbara. She spoke to the old man in German. He looked up. He wore small, round dark glasses which made his gaunt face look almost emaciated. Nevertheless, he was animated, nodded his head vigorously and smiled.

"Mister and Mrs. Turley!" he cried in a surprisingly strong voice. "So good of you! So nice!"

The nurse deposited the chairs and left. He cocked his head to make sure she was gone. When he was satisfied, he produced an enormous cigar from beneath his shawl and lit it, sending clouds of blue smoke into the morning air.

"Like Brahms," he said and chuckled. "My only remaining vice . . . apart from occasional bad temper. Please. Sit. Sit."

Roger and Barbara drew their chairs close and sat down facing him.

"So," he said. "I know you were a student of mine. But I can't remember when."

Roger told him they'd come on behalf of Catherine Macroth. Schneider turned to them in his wheelchair.

"It is true then?" he whispered.

"Apparently."

The old man sat still for awhile, gazing across the lawn at years ago. He shook his head so slowly the movement was almost imperceptible. "Macroth," he murmured. "*Gott.* Such a calamity." He removed his black wafer glasses then and turned his pale blue eyes toward them.

"If ever," he said gently, "you could hear him play *La Grande Pièce Symphonique* you would understand. It is not even César Franck's best work. But when Macroth plays it . . ." He shrugged and looked away. "Also the *Fantasie in A Major* and the *Six Pièces* and the *Pastorale.*" He sighed. "Of course, he plays also *Baroquemusik* as well as Classical and Romantic. In his first year at university, he plays all the Bach chorale preludes . . . and *Der Grösse Fugue* . . . and he makes his own transcription of the Goldberg Variations for baroque organ. All this in his first year, *nicht?*" Schneider tucked the cigar in his mouth and replaced the dark glasses. "The Macroth transcription stays now in the music library at Dalhousie where nobody plays it. It is too difficult except for him."

The cigar went out. He fumbled for his matches and dropped the box on the grass. Roger picked it up and struck a light for him. Schneider heard the match strike and moved the tip of the cigar toward the sound. It was then they saw he was blind. After he took a few puffs he chuckled.

"Nowadays the hearing is much better than the seeing. For an old musician, this is a thoughtful gift from the Almighty." He puffed in silence for awhile. A long cigar ash fell in his lap. He either felt it or heard it, for he brushed it away. "If the nurse catches me smoking," he said, "she unplugs my radio and takes away my morning coffee. She is from Silesia where vindictiveness is a way of life."

Roger laughed and touched the old man's shoulder. This pleased him. He turned to Roger.

"You have heard him play, of course?" he asked.

"Only the piano," Roger said.

"So . . . the piano." He said it the way he might have said "the ukulele." It was a dismissal. "*Ja,*" he went on. "His first instrument is the pianoforte. Because of his uncle. But, although he is capable of virtuoso technique, the piano is not enough for him. It is the organ that serves his genius. And, thanks to God, it is the organ that brings him to me!" He puffed. "Teaching him was . . . a uniqueness. A joy! A jubilation! He devoured the organ literature like a starving man devours thick soup. The organ gave his life . . . *Herrlichkeit.* I forget the English word."

"Grandeur?" Roger guessed.

"*Ja.* Grandeur. He uses that word often. Once, I will tell you, he plays the Toccata in Halifax Cathedral. The pedal trombone of the cathedral organ is thirty-two feet. When Macroth reaches the last page of the Fugue, I think the saints come down from the windows and march up the aisle."

They talked for almost two hours. The old man did not tire. On the contrary, he seemed to derive energy and strength from the reminiscences. Finally, Roger saw the nurse start down the lawn. Somehow, Dr. Schneider knew she was coming and palmed the remains of the cigar butt with an expertise born of long practice. Barbara brushed off one last bit of ash. He nodded his thanks and patted her arm.

The nurse spoke to him in a sort of singing, scolding *Platdeutsch.* He sighed.

"It is time almost for lunch," he said sadly. "I would invite you to stay but it will be cottage cheese and pear halves and nearly not for eating." He held out both his hands. "I am honored and delighted you come this long way to see an old organ grinder." He laughed at his own joke, then, soberly, added, "and to share your pain at this most terrible loss."

It took all of Barbara's willpower to keep from telling him Con was alive.

*"Herr doktor?"* the nurse said and grasped the back of his wheelchair.

*"Eineminute, bitte."* He turned a last time to Roger and Barbara. "You know, when he was at Dalhousie in his final year, Macroth's ambition *ultimat* was to become organist at the Church of Ste. Clothilde in Montreal. There is, at Ste. Clothilde, an Austin-Estey instrument of enormous quality with one hundred fifty rank. There the pedal trombe and open diapason are larger even than Halifax. There are two beautiful eight-foot trompe and two four-foot clarion in the Great. A most distinguished instrument in a glorious church. It is a pity ... and an irony ... that, a few months ago, Macroth could have had that position."

A chill ran down Roger's back and legs. "Dr. Schneider," he said as calmly as he could, "are you saying that the Church of Ste. Clothilde has a new organist?"

*"Ja.* The item appears in *The Etude* and also *The Organ Guild News* which the nurse reads to me. The old organist at Ste. Clothilde, Cavaillé ... a friend of Dupré ... dies in February, I think."

Roger knelt by the wheelchair. "Do you know the name of the new organist?"

Schneider laughed. "My dear fellow," he said, "when you are over ninety, details and names tend to remain ... inaccessible."

"Is his name Kean?" Roger asked. "David Kean?"

The old man leaned forward. He tilted his head to one side. Then with great energy, he made a fist.

*"Ja!* Kean. You know him?"

# CHAPTER 24

"Y ou promised!" Barbara said in the cab.

Roger clapped his hands. "Barbara, we've got him! We know who he is! We know where he is! All we have to do is identify him! The Mounties will do the rest."

She stared out the cab window at the rows of bay-windowed Halifax homes moving slowly behind black-trunked shade trees. She laid her head on the back of the seat to keep the tears from spilling out of her eyes. It didn't help. She turned, then, and pressed her face against his chest.

"I've loved you for so long I can't remember how it was before." He held her and stroked her hair. "I love you," she said, "and I want what you want. But what we're doing now is wrong. I know it!" She looked up at him. "Roger, let's go home. Please!

Not because of Leonetti. Because of Con! The things that old man said nearly broke my heart. We can't do this! Con's an endangered species! We have to let him go free!"

Roger held her tight. He closed his eyes and concentrated on what he honestly believed was right. "No," he said. "The price is too high."

They flew toward the setting sun to Montreal via Québecair. Barbara shut herself in the room at the Hôtel St. Laurent while Roger kept his appointment with RCMP Inspector Bonnier. The appointment had been set up by Cliff Leonard through Egality's office in Ottawa.

Roger was disappointed in Bonnier. The name "Royal Canadian Mounted Police" had a certain ring to it. The name, to Americans at least, betokened trackless wastes in the Northwest Territory, Hudson's Bay, wolves howling just beyond the campfire and, if you were old enough, Nelson Eddy. Gone were the scarlet tunics, the wide-brimmed hats; gone the horses on which the Mounties mounted ... except in Madison Square Garden. Bonnier wore no uniform. He was small and pale with thinning gray hair and a suit to match. He disliked working on Saturdays and had little enthusiasm for this affair.

He pushed a folder across the desk at Roger. "Is that the man?" he asked. The folder contained two photo reproductions of Con: one of a passport picture taken years ago and the other a poorly defined photocopy of the wire-service photograph distributed when he was reported missing.

"Yes," said Roger.

"There's no doubt in your mind?"

"None."

Bonnier retrieved the folder. "You realize he may have changed his mug somewhat? Do you think you'll recognize him with a nose job?"

"Yes," Roger said. "However, since he's only been ashore a month I doubt if he's had time for cosmetic surgery."

Bonnier grunted and studied Roger. "I have several reasons for asking. First. We know a few things about Macroth. He became a Canadian citizen in 1952 when he entered Dalhousie. But, apart from an occasional speeding ticket and one charge of disturbing the peace, he has no record. No record of larceny or embezzlement, blackmail or forgery or any of the dark crimes you now attribute to him." He paused and checked his notes. "While it is true we know nothing about David R. Kean, you will understand there has been no time to check tax, voting or license-bureau files. Even the St. John's Hall of Records," he added peevishly, "is closed on Saturday. In other words, Mr. Truly, all we have against Macroth/Kean is the IDI material supplied by you and an affirmation by the Egality Corporation that the case has merit."

Roger nodded.

"I have a second reason for wishing to be very sure you can give a positive identification." He leaned back in his chair and peered at Roger. "The vestry office at the Church of Ste. Clothilde acknowledges that Kean has been organist at the church for three weeks. They are most impressed by him; most protective. And they are most guarded in giving out any information about him. It seems he has, in less than a month, caused something of a sensation in Montreal music circles. To the fact, therefore, that he is already a person of some distinction . . . almost a cause célèbre . . . add the prestige of the church and its distinguished congregation, and you have a situation which"—he paused and reached for the appropriate phrase—"which must preclude our making a mistake."

Roger realized Bonnier's job was on the line. "I'm sure I'll recognize him," Roger said.

The Protestant Church of Ste. Clothilde was considered a minor masterpiece. It would have been considered a major masterpiece except it was a deliberate copy of Chartres Cathedral. It was no less majestic. Built long before separatism by a consortium of English and French Canadian businessmen at an unprecedented cost, it stood in the center of five choice acres of greensward and white oak in downtown Montreal, a fact that had sent more than one real estate agent into early retirement. The neighborhood was severely zoned against commercial development and the church property itself bulwarked by a wealthy and influential congregation that included several ex-prime ministers.

They had much to be proud of. Ste. Clothilde's masonry and grillwork had been fashioned by European craftsmen especially imported for the task. The stained glass was priceless, particularly as it had been recently enhanced by the acquisition and installation of the magnificent Elskus sunburst in the huge southern facade. The Austin-Esty 152 rank organ, built in 1949–50, was, along with the 160 rank organ at Curtis Institute in Philadelphia, one of the finest instruments in North America. Yet, until now, its potential had hardly been realized. The music at Ste. Clothilde had always been exemplary. Now it was exalted!

Barbara gazed at the great church, sparkling in the first gold rays of the clear Sunday sunrise. She shivered. It was cold. She hadn't slept. She'd crept out of bed before dawn, careful not to disturb Roger, and walked the half mile downtown with the vague idea of going to early service. Maybe Con would be there. Maybe he'd be at the organ and she could warn him. Then she remembered there was no music at early communion. Maybe she could leave a note on the music rack. "Mayday! Mayday!" Maybe she could pray for a miracle: a tiny earthquake that wouldn't hurt anybody but would cancel the service. Ridiculous. She couldn't jiggle the canoe and spoil the hunter's aim the way she had years ago when her older brother had drawn a bead on an unsuspecting doe drinking at the water's edge. It was too late. She couldn't undo what she'd already helped do. She was as responsible as Roger. "Come ye who are truly repentant." She remembered the sweet words. But it was too late now for God's grace. She walked back to the hotel.

Inspector Bonnier met them in the coffee shop at 10:30. He had a schedule. The service of Holy Eucharist was over at 11:52 and the Recessional at 11:55. Kean would play the organ postlude, César Franck's *Chorale in A minor,* starting at 11:56. "Of course the times are approximate," he said, "but we're expected at eleven-fifty."

"Why so late?" Roger asked.

"Father Durhan allows no one in the sacristy passage until after the Eucharist. We have to go through the passage and up a stairwell to reach the room over the sacristy where there's a clear view of the organ."

An RCMP Ford LTD took them to the church arriving at 11:50 as planned. They went into the building through the choir entrance. The sexton led them down an elaborately tiled corridor to a narrow, Gothic doorway of heavy oak. This led to the sacristy. Roger had to duck to get through. They climbed narrow, spiraling granite steps which ended in a small, unfinished maintenance room. One end of the room was completely open to the church chancel but for a dozen decorative wooden columns. They could see and hear the service from here.

The rector was finishing the Benediction.

"May the Lord make his face to shine upon you and give you peace . . . now and forever more."

"Amen," intoned the congregation.

The organ played the introduction to the Recessional Hymn. The crucifer and acolytes rose, moved center, bowed to the cross, turned and led the singing choir, the rector and curate from the chancel. The singing receded. Roger moved to the opening and looked out between the columns. He looked for the organ and saw nothing. The organ was apparently directly beneath them. Inspector Bonnier pointed across the choir stalls to the other side of the chancel. There, fastened to the mahogany molding, was a large mirror, angled to enable the choir on the same side of the chancel as the organist to follow his directions. Roger looked at the mirror and saw the organist.

His head was shaved. His face was gaunt and deeply tanned, the skin stretched tightly, like a drumhead, over the cheekbones. He had a full gray beard. The blue eyes, huge and adrift in the scraggy countenance, roamed over the instrument as he finished the hymn and set up the stops for the postlude. There was no doubt whatever that the organist was Con Macroth.

Roger turned to speak to Inspector Bonnier. But there was a

sudden, silent commotion as members of the choir hurried up the stairway into the small room. In a moment it was packed with hushed, cassocked figures, all vying for a view of the organist. They had come to hear Con play the Franck Chorale. Some even had scores. Barbara took Roger's hand.

The music began. Roger physically recoiled from the attack of sound that struck him; from the assault of peeling, tumbling notes played at breakneck velocity. The sound seemed to be in the same room with him. The notes began to fall and fell until he thought he might fall. Then came an ascending chordal pyramid and a great crescendo. Then silence. The crescendo reverberated to the deepest part of the huge church. Again the tumbling cadenza as the opening bars were repeated. Roger was dazzled. He had never heard anything like this. He glanced at the young man standing next to Barbara. The man's eyes were glazed. He seemed to be holding his breath lest the meter of his breathing interfere with the chorale.

The slow movement began: a broad, romantic wind melody with falling harmonics beneath. It was utterly beautiful, romantic without being sentimental, a melody of longing played with exquisite fluidity and balance.

Roger looked through the open columns at the congregation. The church was packed, with people standing against the rear wall. No one had moved after the Benediction. He saw row after row of rapt faces, some upturned to the great sunburst window, some with eyes closed; all absorbed in the sustaining music. Then he saw Des. Des was in the third pew on the center aisle with his head slightly bowed. He looked asleep. He looked older. His face seemed lined. But, as the final section of the great chorale began with the pedal notes of the huge trombone pipe, Des raised his head and Roger saw the face was not lined but tear-streaked.

The trumpeting dissonances cascaded above the great pedal diapason. The church shook. Roger looked down at the organist. He was exultant! He was in absolute control, hurling thunderclaps of sound! No feat of Cúchulainn, no salmon leap or hero's halo could match this for grandeur!

When it was over no one moved or spoke. Unable to applaud,

the congregation conveyed its esteem by silence and immobility. Finally, reluctantly, figures rose here and there. A rustling, lingering exit began. One by one, the choir filed out of the small maintenance room and down the narrow stairwell to the sacristy passage.

When they were gone, Inspector Bonnier came over to Roger. He glanced down at the mirror as the organist cleared the ranks and turned off the great instrument. The electric motors decelerated. The organ stopped breathing.

"Well, Mr. Truly. Is that the man?"

Roger put his arm around Barbara and held her close. He watched Con extinguish the rack light, remove the music and slide slowly out of the mirror's reflection.

"No, Inspector," Roger said. "That's not the man."